BOOKS by I. A. HOROWITZ

HOW TO THINK AHEAD IN CHESS
(*with Fred Reinfeld*)

CHESS FOR BEGINNERS

WORLD CHESSMASTERS IN BATTLE ROYAL
(*with Hans Kmoch*)

BOOKS by FRED REINFELD

HOW TO THINK AHEAD IN CHESS
(*with I. A. Horowitz*)

THE TREASURY OF CHESS LORE

THE IMMORTAL GAMES OF CAPABLANCA

WINNING CHESS

THE FIRESIDE BOOK OF CHESS
(*with Irving Chernev*)

I. A. HOROWITZ

FRED REINFELD

CHESS TRAPS,

PITFALLS,

AND SWINDLES

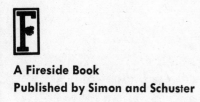

A Fireside Book
Published by Simon and Schuster

ISBN 0-671-21041-6
LIBRARY OF CONGRESS CATALOG CARD NUMBER 54-9790
DEWEY DECIMAL CLASSIFICATION NUMBER 794.1
MANUFACTURED IN THE UNITED STATES OF AMERICA

Contents

PART FOUR

Gimmick *vs.* Gimmick

PART ONE

CHESS GIMMICKS
AND THE PSYCHOLOGY
BEHIND THEM

CHAPTER 1

Even the Masters Can Go Wrong

One of the members of our chess club has a standing gripe. He loves the game, plays avidly, studies a good deal, and tries hard to apply what he's learned. He gets off to a good start in the opening, outplays his opponent and . . . at some point or other, the position turns against him catastrophically. "Why? Why?" he wails.

Recently he called us over to his table. We sat down, and he began setting up the pieces to show us his latest gaffe. "I outplayed him all the way. First I won the Exchange. The duffer had overlooked it. Then I picked up a Pawn. He was just going along on momentum. The extra Pawn was a passed Pawn, well supported by my Queen and Rook. I pushed it right down to the seventh rank. His face was longer than a plank. Here's the position:

(*See Diagram 1.*)

"I have Black, of course. I saw that I could simply queen my Pawn, winning his Rook, with a crushing material advantage. But then I thought, 'Wait a minute! Maybe he has something up his sleeve. Suppose I queen the Pawn—is there anything he can do?' I stole a quick look at him, without lifting my head. No, he sat there with a hang-dog expression. So I moved the Pawn to the eighth, and reached out for a new Queen. Suddenly he let out an ear-splitting whoop, banged down the Queen to King

Diagram 1 (*Black to play*)

eight, screaming 'CHECK,' and laughing like a banshee. Would you believe it, I'd gone and done it again! Two Queens ahead after I take his Queen off, but he answers Rook takes Rook and I'm mated! Is that justice, I ask you?!"

The answer is, Yes, of course that's justice. You don't win the game until you win it. Any last-minute slip, any momentary negligence, any fatigue, any overconfidence, any greed, any underestimation of your opponent—all or any of these can turn your prospective victory into defeat. Sometimes, in the grip of despair that such mishaps bring on, we wonder whether there aren't two kinds of chess—our own, spotty, improvised, and inconsistent; and that of the masters, flawless, foresighted, and ever logical.

But at this point we needn't despair. The masters are admittedly magnificent chessplayers. But it is far from true that all their games are examples of pure reason and inhuman perfection. The masters, too, can go wrong. Personal motives play a big role in their games. Vanity, time pressure, caprice, poor judgment, oversights, miscalculation, and all the other ills that chessplayers' flesh is heir to, appear in their games.

Sounds incredible? Well, let's see some of our grandmasters in action. Here is a position in which Alexander Alekhine (whom we consider the greatest player in the history of the game) blundered miserably.

(*See Diagram 2.*)

ALEKHINE

Diagram 2 (*Black to play*)

BUERGER

Black is a Pawn to the good; he has outplayed his opponent completely; his Bishops are all-powerful. By playing 1 . . . N—N5 he can pretty well reduce White to a state of helplessness. Instead, we get this fantastic sequel—and this is the actual play:

1 . . . .   N—B5??

A gruesome blunder.

2 PxN   BxN

So far, so good. But the great Alekhine has completely overlooked his opponent's forking reply, which wins a piece.

3 N—N3   QxP??

A second blunder, and an even more gruesome one. He is blind to the possibility of 4 N—R5*ch*, forking the Black King and Queen.

4 NxB?   . . . .

And White is blind too! He fails to find the fork, being content to win the piece and, in due course, the game. Of course there was a reason for this wretched play—grueling time pressure. Each player had only a few seconds for his remaining moves before the time control. The point we are stressing here is: you see a grand master, perhaps the greatest of them all, with his wits quite addled because he has to play a few rapid moves in an easily won position.

Incidentally, it isn't always the player at the board who goes wrong. Sometimes you come across notes written by a commentator who presumably had ample time—yet not enough to save him from a ludicrous blunder. Here is an amusing example:

TEICHMANN

Diagram 3 (*Black to play*)

VIDMAR

Teichmann was blind in one eye, but he had a keen sight of the board just the same. Having given up the Exchange in return for a Pawn, he is somewhat at a material disadvantage. After a careful study of the position, he played 1 . . . R—KN3.

Tarrasch, at that time (1907) one of the world's greatest masters, annotated this game for a newspaper column. Ridiculing Teichmann's move, he pointed out that "of course 1 . . . QxP was the right move. If then 2 QxBP, R—Q3!; 3 RxR??, P—K7! and Black wins on the spot!" Tarrasch added a number of sarcastic remarks and some involved variations which we need not go into here. His note was copied in columns and magazines the world over, with no dissenting voice.

Only when the Book of the Tournament (Carlsbad, 1907) appeared several years later, did the chess world find out what

Teichmann had seen with his one good eye. The fact is that Diagram 3 is the setting for a particularly devilish pitfall that Vidmar has set for his opponent. Tarrasch quite overlooked that *1 . . .* QxP?? is a fearful blunder. Here is what would happen (from Diagram 3):

1	QxP??
2 QxPch!!	NxQ
3 R—Q8ch	N—B1
4 R—R8ch!!	KxR
5 RxN mate!	

So you see that even a first-rate master, with all the time in the world at his disposal, can fall into a carefully baited trap. Traps—traps like this one—form the subject matter of this book. How to set them. How to see through them. How to parry them.

One particularly painful kind of trap is the one that a player sets when he has a lost game. If his opponent, well on the way to victory, succumbs, then he loses all the fruits of his previous good play. Such a trap, if successful, we shall term a "swindle." Incidentally, there is nothing unethical or immoral or illegal about a chess "swindle." We use it here as a technical term to distinguish a certain kind of trap.

GROB

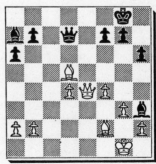

Diagram 4 (*Black to play*)

FLOHR

In Diagram 4 you see a "swindle" of the most blatant kind which caught a great master completely off guard:

Black is a Pawn down with no compensation. In the natural course of events he is bound to lose the game because of this material disadvantage. This is all the more certain because he is playing one of the world's leading masters.*

Desperately Grob tries a swindle. He plays:

1 . . . .   **Q—N4!?**

Flohr thinks . . . and thinks . . . and resigns! Why?

He sees that Black threatens 2 . . . Q—B8 mate. True, the mate can be stopped by 2 Q—K1 or 2 Q—N1, but in that case Black replies 2 . . . QxB winning a piece and threatening 3 . . . Q—N7 mate. As there is no defense, Flohr resigns.

But wait . . . *is* there really no defense after *1* . . . Q—N4, that murderous-looking move with a twofold threat? Indeed there is a defense, a perfectly simple one—though, alas, not an obvious one. The refutation of *1* . . . Q—N4 is:

2 **K—R1!!**   . . . .

This King move breaks the spell woven by Black's threats. The delightful point is that if *2* . . . Q—B8*ch;* *3* B—N1. The White King is snug, and White can go on to win more material.

But of course mere printed analysis can never reproduce the feelings and reactions of living players in a real game. Logical analysis tells us nothing of the terror and panic that must have paralyzed Flohr's customarily clear thinking. Like a magician, Black created an overwhelming illusion with *1* . . . Q—N4!? Such black magic plays an important role in chess.

But illusions are not always created by the opponent. Sometimes a player creates his own illusions—or delusions. The greatest masters have such lapses, and even World Championship contests are not free from them. The United States Champion-

---

* No longer true today. It *was* true in 1933, when this game was played.

ship Tournament of 1951 produced a remarkable instance of "chess blindness."

PAVEY

Diagram 5 (*Black to play*)

HOROWITZ

Black, one of the finest players in the country, has completely outplayed his opponent. Two Pawns and the Exchange ahead, Black also has a passed Queen Knight Pawn which is free to saunter down to the eighth rank and become a Queen. Why hasn't White resigned? For one thing, he remembers Tartakover's excellent dictum: "Nobody ever won a game of chess by resigning."

White sees a microscopic possibility of escaping defeat. Suppose Black, in his search for the clearest and simplest winning line, overreaches himself? Twice earlier in the tournament Black had missed easy wins when his opponents saved themselves by a perpetual check. Troubled by the recollection of these mishaps, Black rules out all danger—so he thinks—by playing:

> 1 . . . .   **QxBch??**

With this bit of sham elegance Black succumbs to the very danger he was trying to avoid.

> **2 QxQ**   **R—R6**

And now White has a fantastic resource that saves the game:

3 K—R4!!   RxQ

Forced, of course. But now White is stalemated!!

PAVEY

Diagram 6
(*White to play*)

HOROWITZ

"White to play," the diagram caption reads. But White has no moves whatever, and the game ends in a draw.

Cases of a player going wrong because he is trying too hard to be careful happen more often than you might suppose. But

RESHEVSKY

Diagram 7
(*White to play*)

PILNICK

carelessness is a much more frequent contributing factor. Even Sammy Reshevsky, the country's outstanding player, can become careless during the course of a game that has already gone 91 weary moves! Exceptionally industrious and imperturbable, Sammy plays 100-move games with the same zest that the rest of us reserve for 10-second chess. So it comes as something of a shock to learn that even Sammy can go wrong.

After 91 moves of play in another United States Championship Tournament (1942), White finds himself three Pawns down in a hopelessly lost ending. Just before resigning, he tries a million-to-one shot:

1 Q—KB5!   . . . .

This has gone far enough, says Black to himself, and plays:

1 . . . .   P—N5??

Played on the principle of "anything will do." The idea is that after 2 QxP??, Q—K8ch and 3 . . . Q—N6ch forces the exchange of Queens, with an easily won King and Pawn ending. And, of course, if White refuses the offered Pawn, the Black King-side Pawns advance victoriously.

Black's reasoning in the preceding paragraph is impeccable—with the exception of that dangerous phrase, "of course." White finds the flaw:

2 Q—KB2!!   QxQ

He must take! But now White is stalemated! (*Diagram* 8)

The "chess gimmicks" we discuss in this book are traps, pitfalls, and swindles. As we shall deal with quite a few examples of each, let us first define them.

RESHEVSKY

Diagram 8
(*White to play*)

PILNICK

We use the term *trap* in a somewhat specialized sense—for situations where a player goes wrong by his own efforts. He is confronted with a critical choice, and for one reason or another—greed, carelessness, fatigue, overanxiety, miscalculation—he makes the wrong choice. In Diagram 5 you have an instance of a trap: Black can win in a variety of ways. Instead, he chooses 1 . . . QxBch?? and thus blunders away the win.

Pitfalls are another story. Here the "beneficiary," the man who will profit by a blunder, plays an active role. He conceives a plausible position in which a guileless move by his opponent will turn out badly. Thereupon the "beneficiary" or "trap-setter" makes the move that gives his opponent a chance to go wrong.

In Diagram 16 you will see how a pitfall works: White plays 6 PxP, allowing the proper reply 6 . . . PxP and the faulty reply 6 . . . NxP??? Black plays 6 . . . NxP???, which looks safe, even strong—and finds himself checkmated only three moves later.

A *swindle* is a special form of the pitfall. A swindle is a pitfall adopted by a player who has a clearly lost game. If his opponent sees the idea and avoids it, the losing player . . . loses. If his opponent misses the point, the losing player is rescued from despair, and manages to draw—or even win!

Diagram 7 is a fine example of a swindle. There you saw how White played 1 Q—KB5! with a hope and a prayer that his opponent, a player of World Championship caliber, would overlook an elementary idea mentioned in most chess primers. Had Black seen through his opponent's intentions, he could have smashed the flimsy swindle in a variety of ways (1 . . . Q—B5, for example). But Black missed the point, and the swindle worked as planned (2 Q—KB2!!).

So there they are—the trap, the pitfall, and the swindle. Though ignored in virtually all chess books, they play an enormously important role in over-the-board chess, and decide the fate of countless games.

CHAPTER 2

More About Traps, Pitfalls, and Swindles

Some people say that human nature never changes. Be that as it may, the perennial chess traps, though old as the hills, still retain their power to befuddle the minds of chessplayers. The aptly named Fool's Mate is a case in point. In its original form chess, as the ancient Indians, Persians, and Arabs played it, made the Queen the weakest piece on the chessboard, being empowered to move only one square in any direction.

Then, during the Middle Ages, a blow was struck for women's rights, and the Queen became the strongest piece on the board. We can imagine chessplayers of that time having trouble getting used to seeing the Queen zoom right across the board, making long-distance captures, and creating fantastic threats from remote points. Many a duffer in those days must have fallen victim to the Fool's Mate:

1 P—KB3?	P—K4
2 P—KN4???	Q—R5 mate

This is a classic trap theme—an inept player opening lines leading to his King and being checkmated with shocking rapidity. But tyros are not the only ones guilty of neglecting the King's welfare. In fact, not so many years ago one of the authors of this book found himself taken in by a particularly embarrassing variant of the Fool's Mate theme.

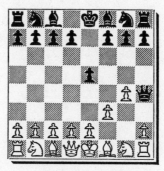

Diagram 9

FOOL'S MATE!

At the Manhattan Chess Club Horowitz often played with an arch-duffer known as a "professional Rook-odds player." Always receiving odds of a Rook, Mr. P.R.O.P. was willing to play for any stakes his opponent might name. His main ambition in life was to improve his chess to the point where the masters would ignore his arrival at the club.

That happy day never came. In fact, whenever Mr. P.R.O.P. entered the club rooms, the pros vied with each other to be the first to get him. Some even went so far as to greet him before he came into the club.

One day Mr. P.R.O.P. walked in; and immediately singled out Horowitz.

"I have a proposition for you," he said. "I'd like to play at the usual odds for a stake of ten dollars." Nothing new in this; but then Mr. P.R.O.P. went on:

"During the course of the game, at any time I don't like *your* move, I'll suggest a different one. Every time you take back *your* move and play the move *I* suggest, I give you a dollar. On the other hand, if you refuse my suggestion, it costs you nothing."

After a moment's thought, Horowitz agreed. What could he lose? The game proceeded: *

1 P—Q4   N—KB3

* In setting up the pieces to play over this game, remember that White is playing without his Queen Rook!

P.R.O.P.

Diagram 10
(*White to play*)

HOROWITZ

Horowitz played 2 P—K3, whereupon his blackhearted opponent commented, "Capablanca generally plays 2 N—Q2, instead of 2 P—K3. Play 2 N—Q2, instead of the move you've made, and you get a dollar."

"If it's good enough for Capa, it's good enough for me," Horowitz replied, putting the King Pawn back on its original square and continuing with:

2 **N—Q2**   . . . .

For some mysterious reason Mr. P.R.O.P. seemed very gratified by Horowitz's accommodating change of mind. Equally mysterious was his reply:

2 . . . .   **P—K4**

What surprised Horowitz about this move was that it was the first time in the history of chess, as far as he knew, that a Rook-odds player had willingly parted with a Pawn.

Horowitz's first thought was to take the Pawn; but then it occurred to him that this was the move that Mr. P.R.O.P. wanted. Why waste a dollar? So Horowitz craftily played the timid 3 P—K3, producing the expected reaction from Mr. P.R.O.P.

"If you take the King Pawn instead, you can have another dollar!"

No sooner said than done. Horowitz put the King Pawn back on its original square a second time and played:

3 PxP   . . . .

To which the reply was:

3 . . . .   **N—N5**

P.R.O.P.

Diagram 11
(*White to play*)

HOROWITZ

Horowitz played **4 KN—B3,** developing a piece and guarding the advanced King Pawn. Again the Rook-odds player had a suggestion.

"If you take back your last move," came the soft insinuating voice of Satan, "and play **4 P—KR3** instead, you can have another dollar."

At this point Horowitz's suspicions were belatedly aroused. What was the point of so much generosity? Perhaps, he said to himself, he wants me to play **4 P—KR3** so that he can answer **4 . . . NxBP.** But the sacrifice would be silly—just a check or two by the Black Queen, and then Black has nothing.

Perhaps, Horowitz continued, he just wants to be sure of winning₊the King Pawn. That's more like it! After all, you can expect a Rook-odds player to think like a Rook-odds player. That's it!—he wants the King Pawn.

And so Horowitz agreed to put back his King Knight on KN1 and earn a dollar by playing:

4 P—KR3???   . . . .

Three dollars to the good and smugly awaiting further windfalls, Horowitz was rudely awakened by Mr. P.R.O.P.'s next move:

4 . . . .   **N—K6!!**

P.R.O.P.

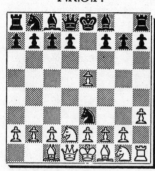

Diagram 12
(*White to play*)

HOROWITZ

Too late, much too late, Horowitz realized that his opponent's last suggestion was not a windfall but a pitfall! If White plays **5 PxN,** he runs into *5 . . . Q—R5ch; 6 P—KN3, QxNP mate.* (Note the similarity to our old friend the Fool's Mate—Diagram 9.)

So, to the accompaniment of thunderous guffaws at his expense, poor Horowitz could do nothing better than resort to **5 KN—B3, NxQ; 6 KxN,** which left him with the overwhelming material disadvantage of a Knight against Queen and Rook.*

* Not so overwhelming against a Rook-odds player. To complete the saga of Horowitz's downfall via a windfall that was really a pitfall, we must record that he finally won the game!

This is a good point at which to review the difference between a trap and a swindle. The Fool's Mate (Diagram 9) is clearly a trap, because White plays himself into a mating situation without any active assistance or provocation from his opponent.

In the amusing little game that we have just played over, however, each suggestion proffered by Mr. P.R.O.P. harbors a possible pitfall. His suggested moves may be perfectly safe—or they may be catastrophic. Of course, this privilege of suggesting moves out loud is most unusual. Nevertheless, in a game of chess there are many moves that challenge, provoke, tempt; a game is after all an unspoken dialogue, and the move that leads to a pitfall is expressed just as clearly and sharply as if its meaning were set forth in words.

Consider, for example, this pitfall from the Gruenfeld Defense starting from the following opening sequence:

1	P—Q4	N—KB3
2	P—QB4	P—KN3
3	N—QB3	P—Q4
4	PxP	NxP
5	P—K4	NxN
6	PxN	P—QB4
7	B—QB4	B—N2

Even at this early stage you can see that a fierce fight is shaping up for mastery of the center. If White's Queen Pawn can hold out against the pressure on the long diagonal, then the game will be in White's favor. If Black's pressure on the Pawn cannot be neutralized, then the advantage will definitely be with Black.

8	N—K2	N—B3
9	B—K3	PxP
10	PxP	Q—R4ch
11	B—Q2	. . . .

Black's Queen is attacked. Should he play safe and retreat the Queen, or should he take the risky course of maintaining the offensive by playing the Queen to QR6? At QR6 the Black

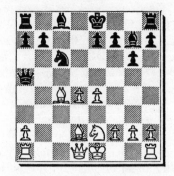

Diagram 13 (*Black to play*)

Queen will be dangerously exposed to threats by White's pieces. On the other hand, White's Queen Pawn is menaced and White will have to lose some time defending it. So:

11 . . . .   Q—R6!

Now White is faced with the problem of guarding the Queen Pawn.

He can, if he wishes, solve the problem drastically by setting a pitfall with 12 P—Q5!? Then, if Black snaps at the Rook with 12 . . . BxR? there follows 13 QxB attacking Black's King Rook and still keeping Black's Knight under attack.

Clearly this would not do as far as Black is concerned. Black would therefore answer 12 P—Q5!? with 12 . . . N—K4; and after 13 B—QN5ch, N—Q2 White would be faced with the loss of his Queen Rook Pawn after the forced move of his Queen Rook.

White does not relish these complications, so he chooses a crafty alternative which sets two refined pitfalls, seemingly without risk:

12 QR—N1?!   . . . .

White is defending his Queen Pawn indirectly by means of a pitfall: 12 . . . NxP??; 13 B—N4 winning the Queen. Like a sudden flash of lightning this variation lights up the dangers to which Black has exposed himself by the apparently wayward moves of his Queen.

Diagram 14 (*Black to play*)

And the second pitfall? In reply to an indifferent move by Black, White plans 13 P—Q5, N moves; 14 B—N4 winning the Black Queen. Black is seemingly unaware of the danger.

12	**Castles!**
13 P—Q5	. . . .

He carries out his plan.

13	**N—K4!**

Black is unafraid, for he relies on a magnificent pitfall of his own.

14 B—N4?	. . . .

Crushing as this move looks, it does *not* trap Black's Queen!

14	**Q—KB6!!**

Plotting Black's downfall, White has only achieved a disaster for himself.

Overwhelmed by Black's surprise move, White quickly capitulates: *

* White can avoid immediate loss by 15 Castles, but after *15 . . . QxKP* his game is hopeless.

Diagram 15
(*White to play*)

15	PxQ??	NxPch
16	K—B1	B—R6 mate!

The pitfalls in this brief game bear out what was said earlier about moves that are part of an unspoken dialogue. The pitfall moves challenge and provoke; a sparkling, witty struggle rages about the worth or worthlessness of the pitfall moves. This is chess at its best and most interesting—the sharp clash of two resourceful personalities.

We observed earlier that the classic trap themes are old as the hills. One such favorite motif is the sensational breaking of an apparently invincible pin. Traps and pitfalls are the enemies of routine and the cliché; they introduce the element of the unexpected, enabling creative originality to triumph over moldy principles.

Few principles are more reliable in chess than the one which emphasizes the restraining effect of a pin. Every player who has ever been subjected to the crippling power of a pin rejoices to see a pin broken by the delightful stratagem named for the Sieur de Légal, who was the teacher of Philidor, the greatest master of the eighteenth century. It is said that as a youngster Philidor succumbed to this pitfall while playing against Légal. Involving as it does the sacrifice of the most valuable piece on the chessboard, the Légal pitfall is both spectacular and useful.

The pitfall has appeared in a number of forms, the most familiar being:

1	P—K4	P—K4
2	N—KB3	N—QB3
3	B—B4	P—Q3
4	N—B3	P—KR3?
5	P—Q4	B—N5
6	PxP	. . . .

Diagram 16 (*Black to play*)

It is White's last move that sets up the pitfall. Black is at a dangerous crossroads. By playing the prosaic 6 . . . PxP! he would remain perfectly safe. But, relying on the pin, he chooses the bolder and more aggressive alternative:

6	. . . .	NxP??
7	NxN!!	. . . .

A blunder, thinks Black, and gleefully pounces on the Queen.*

7	. . . .	BxQ
8	BxPch	K—K2
9	N—Q5 mate!	

The Légal mate—a pretty picture!

* Black can avoid an immediate mate only at the cost of a piece—7 . . . PxN; 8 QxB. This would almost be equivalent to resigning.

Diagram 17

Venerable as it is, the Légal pitfall is still doing business despite the passage of centuries. It has appeared in thousands of simultaneous exhibitions and—what is even more remarkable—quite a few games between first-class masters.

The Légal stratagem appears, for example, in thinly disguised form in a Ruy Lopez played by Tarrasch and Tchigorin in their match in 1893:

1	P—K4	P—K4
2	N—KB3	N—QB3
3	B—N5	P—QR3
4	B—R4	N—B3
5	N—B3	B—N5
6	N—Q5	B—R4?
7	Castles	P—QN4
8	B—N3	P—Q3
9	P—Q3	B—KN5
10	P—B3	N—K2?

This is the blunder that permits White's winning sacrifice. As Black walks into a lost game voluntarily, without any goading or guiding on White's part, it is proper to speak of this example as a trap and not a pitfall.

White's reply comes as a staggering surprise:

11 NxKP!!   . . . .

TCHIGORIN

Diagram 18
(*White to play*)

TARRASCH

The first point is that if *11 . . . BxQ?; 12 NxNch, PxN??; 13 BxPch, K—B1; 14 B—R6 mate!*

Or if *11 . . . BxQ?; 12 NxNch, K—B1; 13* either *N—Q7ch, QxN* (forced); *14 NxQch, K—K1; 15 RxB, KxN; 16 BxP* and White has won two Pawns.

11	PxN
12 NxNch	PxN
13 QxB	N—N3

The trap winds up with a minor pitfall: Black dare not regain his Pawn with *13 . . . QxP??* because of *14 R—Q1* and wins.

After *13 . . . N—N3* White remains a Pawn to the good and Black's King-side is smashed beyond repair.

The trap was hard to see through because the attacking diagonal of White's Bishop on QN3 was masked by White's Knight at Q5. In addition, the flight square at KB1 for Black's King blinded Tchigorin to the critical nature of the position. Nevertheless, it remains a psychological puzzle that Tchigorin, one of the greatest combinative masters of all time, fell into this trap.

Still another amusing example of a violently broken pin appears in a King's Gambit Declined played by Spielmann and Hromadka at Pistyan, 1922:

1 P—K4	P—K4
2 P—KB4	B—B4
3 N—KB3	P—Q3
4 B—B4	N—QB3
5 P—Q3	N—B3
6 N—B3	B—KN5

The pin!

7 N—QR4	P—QR3
8 NxB	PxN
9 P—QR4	N—KR4
10 P—B5	N—B5
11 Castles	N—Q5?

HROMADKA

Diagram 19
(White to play)

SPIELMANN

Again Black has thoughtlessly relied on the power of the pin, without carefully examining the position. Punishment is speedy:

12 BxPch!	. . . .

For if 12 . . . KxB?; 13 NxPch followed by 14 NxB and White is two Pawns ahead.

12	K—B1
13 BxN	PxB
14 B—R2	. . . .

White won easily with his material and positional advantage. In Part Two we shall see many repetitions of the same idea in springing successful traps and pitfalls.

While we admire the desperate ingenuity that goes into a first-rate swindle, we must also marvel at the impatience of players who let victory slip through their fingers. One master at a famous chess club went so far in his feverish impatience to win that he never even bothered to console a defeated opponent with a polite "You did nobly" or something of that sort. Such conduct was too sissified.

Instead the master would bellow, "Too late!" to indicate his annoyance over the waste of his valuable time by a second-rater. In the following position, the master was all prepared for his usual summation.

Diagram 20
(*White to play*)

With two Pawns up, Black has an easy win. He menaces . . . P—B7 and . . . P—B8, promoting the passed Pawn to a Queen; and for good measure he threatens . . . K—N6, winning the lone White Pawn.

On the brink of resigning, White thinks of a delightful swindle. And so, with a languid, what-difference-does-it-make air, he plays:

1 K—B4!   . . . .

Now if Black takes a minute's thought to see through the swindle, he can win with 1 . . . R—B5*ch,* driving White's King away. (If you don't see the need for this, the following play will make the point clear!)

1 . . . .   P—B7???

Eager to wind up the game, Black heedlessly rushes on to his doom:

2 R—R3*ch!!*   PxR
3 P—N3 mate!

Black has transformed a creditable win into a shameful loss.

Diagram 21

Let this position be a warning to all impatient would-be winners!

_____

CHAPTER 3

Baiting the Trap

In every chess gimmick you will find a paradox imbedded: the victim of the gimmick succumbs because he is following some general principle, some basic idea, some broad postulate. He falls into the trap because he is "following the rules." At the same time, he is unknowingly violating some other principle or overlooking an exception to the rule on which he relies.

The gimmick is the exception, the little quirk that makes a position "different." It can turn up in the simplest positions, in the most harmless-looking ones. It can deprive a player of a well-earned victory at the last minute (as in Diagram 20); it can ruin his game at the very start (Diagram 9). The gimmick makes planning difficult, because it has no inherent connection with a strategic plan. You may be the best planner in the world, but if you follow your plan dogmatically, you may never attain your strategic goal.

How to apply these gimmicks, how to carry them out, how to see through them, how to repulse them or even top them with a better gimmick is the subject of this book. Though average players succumb most readily to gimmicks, the masters set them more often. Their fellow masters usually see through the gimmicks—but not always!

There is much to be learned from these gimmicks and from the psychology behind them. Let us look at several positions and see if there is any factor that is common to them all.

LEVENFISH and
FREYMANN

Diagram 22
(*White to play*)

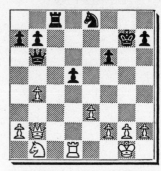

ALEKHINE *and* ESSER

This position turned up in a consultation game played in 1911. White has a clearly won game, with a Pawn to the good and attacking prospects against Black's exposed King.

Thus, White's *long-range* plan calls for attack on the Black King. That Black's isolated Queen Pawn can be captured is irrelevant to the plan, but its removal would give White an overwhelming material advantage. The Pawn is unguarded; hence its capture is attractive. Yet White's capture of the Pawn would lose at once:

1 RxP??   QxNP!!

Now Black wins! For example:
2 QxQ, R—B8*ch* and mate follows.
Or 2 R—Q2, QxQ; 3 RxQ, R—B8 *mate*.

The flaw in White's hasty capture here is that *his first rank is vulnerable to a mating attack*. In capturing the Pawn he is following the principle that it is advantageous to win material, but he is overlooking the all-important principle that it is ruinous to allow a mating attack.

(In the actual play from Diagram 22, White continued *1* N—B3—intensifying the attack on the Queen Pawn and ruling out mating attacks along the Queen Bishop file—and 2 P—KR3,

LEVENFISH *and*
FREYMANN

Diagram 23
(*White to play*)

ALEKHINE *and* ESSER

creating a loophole for the White King and thus safeguarding him against any potential mating attack on the first rank. Note the difference between this careful, sensible policy and Black's headlong blundering in Diagram 20.)

On the other hand, Diagram 24 shows White falling into a pitfall set by his wily opponent. A crisis has resulted from the hot fight over Black's far advanced Queen Bishop Pawn.

CAPABLANCA

Diagram 24
(*White to play*)

BERNSTEIN

White attacks the Queen Bishop Pawn three times, while it is defended twice. As far as mere arithmetic is concerned, the Pawn is doomed. But more than arithmetic is involved, and White owes it to himself to check the position for hidden possibilities. Instead, he plays:

1 NxBP???   . . . .

White embarks on this move not only because arithmetic favors him, but also because he has prepared an extremely subtle pitfall for Black. Unfortunately for White, his opponent's pitfall is the better of the two.

1	NxN
2 RxN	RxR
3 RxR	. . . .

CAPABLANCA

Diagram 25 (*Black to play*)

BERNSTEIN

Here is the crucial point. White expects 3 . . . Q—N8*ch?*; 4 Q—B1, R—Q8???; 5 R—B8*ch* and Black is mated on the following move.

But Black is on an altogether different tack:

3 . . . .   Q—N7!!!
Resigns!

Only now does White discover how wrong he has been. If *4 QxQ, R—Q8 mate.* Or if *4 Q—K1, QxR!; 5 QxQ, R—Q8ch* and mate follows.

After following the play from Diagrams 22 and 24, we can derive a general law about pitfalls.

A pitfall is based on a tactical weakness in the opponent's position. Sometimes the flaw exists before the pitfall begins; in such cases the pitfall is often inspired by the existing weakness. In other positions, the flaw is *provoked* by the pitfall. In Diagrams 22 and 24 we have examples of the former; in the following diagram we see how the other kind operates.

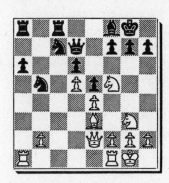

Diagram 26
(*White to play*)

1 N—R5 . . . .

This is a fine example of the purely provocative pitfall.

Black sees that he can fork both Knights by playing . . . P—N3?? As it happens, . . . P—N3?? is a terrible blunder because of the forking reply *N—B6ch* winning Black's Queen.

Simple as this example is, we can learn a great deal about the mechanics of pitfalls from it.

Sometimes a pitfall is an end in itself; at other times it is incidental to the execution of a plan. Here we have the second case: White wanted to post his Knights aggressively, well into the enemy territory. The pitfall was by no means the main object of his plan.

To set such pitfalls is an important feature of chessplaying skill, but it carries its own dangers. Once you have set a pitfall of this kind, you must watch the changing position alertly from move to move, to make sure that what was previously impossible has not suddenly become perfectly feasible.

Now look at it from the victim's point of view (after 1 . . . P—N3??; 2 N—B6ch from Diagram 26). His 1 . . . P—N3?? is pathetically inept, as far as the end-result is concerned. But as in our discussion of Diagram 23, we see here the clash of two principles; one of them ("it is good play to fork two minor pieces") rates far below the other ("it is even better play to fork King and Queen").

And so it is small comfort to Black that his 1 . . . P—N3?? is all right *in principle.* It is all wrong in *application.* Unfortunately, there are some tactical possibilities (here . . . P—N3?? is one of them) that are almost hypnotic in their insidious attractiveness.

Diagram 27 (*Black to play*)

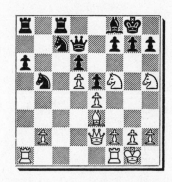

In this position it was Black's duty to ask himself how White proposed to answer the forking move. "Of course I can fork the Knights. But it can't be that easy! How will he answer? Has he just left a piece *en prise* without a constructive idea, without a threat? Can either Knight make a move so dangerous that I

won't be able to capture the remaining one? Can he *check?* Can
he threaten any of my pieces?"

We said that . . . P—N3?? was almost hypnotic in its effect
on Black. Yet with a little common-sense skepticism on his part,
and an obvious question or two, the spell is easily broken.

You will often find that skepticism is particularly called for in
the case of pitfalls set to facilitate a player's development of his
pieces. The point is well illustrated in this position from a game
played at Scheveningen in 1913:

ENGLUND

Diagram 28
(*White to play*)

LASKER

White has a considerable lead in development. This spells
danger for Black, in view of the fact that his King has not yet
castled and is therefore vulnerable to attack along the King file.

In order to profit by his lead in development, White sets a
diabolical pitfall with:

1 QxP!!   . . . .

Now Black can grab the Bishop with his Queen—or he can
turn a long, hard suspicious look at the position. "If I take the
Bishop, what can he do? Does he have a fork, a pin, another
sacrifice? Above all, does he have a *check?*" This line of question-

ing will always lay bare the anatomy of a pitfall. For a *pitfall must be based on a check or a capture or a brutal threat.* A pitfall can function only by means of some such violent method.

ENGLUND

Diagram 29 (*Black to play*)

LASKER

What do you suppose Black's examination of the position yields? With mingled horror and satisfaction he finds that *1 . . . QxB??* would be fatal for him—he is horrified at the thought of his narrow escape, and satisfied because he discovered the danger in time.

Had Black lunged at the bait with *1 . . . QxB??* White planned *2 B—N5ch!, K—B1;* * *3 Q—Q8ch!!, BxQ; 4 R—K8 mate!*

Forewarned in time, Black played:

1 . . . .   **P—B3**

Thus Black has avoided the pitfall—at the cost of a Pawn, it is true. Aside from its ingenuity, this was an excellent pitfall; even when refused, it added to White's advantage. He simply retreated *2 Q—K4,* with a Pawn ahead and a pleasantly increased lead in development.

Thus the pitfall was only incidental to White's general plan; and this is generally true of all pitfalls to facilitate development.

___

* The alternative *2 . . . P—QB3* is refuted by *3 BxPch, PxB; 4 QxQBPch* followed by *5 QxR* and White wins easily.

If the victim stumbles into the pitfall, White wins at once. If he
sees through the pitfall, White still achieves his objective.

You can see how these ideas work out in actual play from the
position reached five moves later in the same game:

ENGLUND

Diagram 30
(*White to play*)

LASKER

White's command of the board has increased noticeably,
and Black is more uneasy than ever about the position of his
King in the center. Well aware of this anxiety, White sets up a
crafty pitfall to keep Black from castling—or to annihilate him if
he does castle.

1 R—Q1!!   . . . .

This subtle move is if anything even more venomous than
White's procedure in Diagram 28. But this time Black can no
longer maintain his cool, inquiring attitude. His position has become worse and worse and he is a beaten man. So he plays precisely the move he ought to avoid:

1	Castles???
2 QxPch!!!	PxQ
3 B—R6 mate!	

What is extraordinarily interesting about the play in Diagrams
28 and 30 is that it is a matter of life or death for Black whether

or not his Queen is actively taking part in the defense. In Diagram 28 he was careful *not to let his Queen wander far afield.* In Diagram 30, however, Black failed to consider the effect of castling without enjoying the active support of the Queen.

This reminds us of another feature of Queen play which, despite its importance, is often neglected by the ordinary player. We all know that the Queen is the strongest piece on the chessboard. But what we forget, or fail to realize, is that this powerful piece should not be lightly sent on trifling expeditions to some remote spot on the board.

The Queen is so important a piece that her loss is for all practical purposes as bad as being checkmated. Time-robbing expeditions with the Queen have resulted in many spectacular pitfalls leading to loss of Her Majesty. Here is an example from a match game played in 1909:

MARSHALL

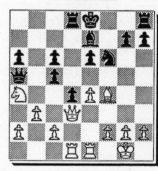

Diagram 31
(*White to play*)

CAPABLANCA

Black's Queen is off to the side and has little influence on the future course of the game. Black will do well to iron out this defect in his position.

But meanwhile White has a problem: he wants to play N—N2, in order to follow up with N—B4, giving the Knight an ideal, unassailable post, as it cannot be driven off by Black Pawns.

An admirable plan as far as strategy is concerned; but what about the tactical aspect? On *1 N—N2* Black plays . . . **QxP** winning a Pawn and gaining time by attacking the Knight. Nevertheless Capablanca, that master of tactical play, blandly continues:

1 **N—N2!**   . . . .

Marshall, an equally great tactician, is too shrewd to stumble blindly into Capablanca's pitfall. A catastrophe would result from:

1 . . . .   **QxP??**
2 **N—B4!**   . . . .

Diagram 32 (*Black to play*)

An amusing position. Black's Queen is trapped on QR7 as firmly as a fly on flypaper and cannot budge. White will calmly follow up with 3 **R—R1** and win the Queen. (In the actual game Marshall avoided this pitfall by answering *1* **N—N2!** with *1* . . . **N—R4**. Nevertheless, Capablanca maintained a marked superiority in position. Thus we have here another instance of a pitfall which is incidental to the execution of a long-range plan.)

In a later game between these famous masters, the roles were reversed. Marshall set the pitfall and Capablanca avoided it. In this game, played in the New York Tournament of 1918, the following position was reached:

(*See Diagram 33.*)

CAPABLANCA

Diagram 33
(*White to play*)

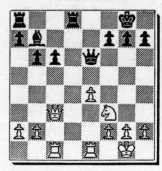

MARSHALL

Black threatens . . . QxRP. Most players would automatically reply *1 P—QR3;* but Marshall, a natural-born attacker, always tried to answer a threat with another threat. His move is:

1 N—Q4!   . . . .

The pitfall! If now *1 . . . QxRP??; 2 R—R1* winning the Queen. Naturally Capablanca sees the pitfall; he must withdraw the Queen, losing time in the process, while White has posted his Knight aggressively and actually gained time! Here again you see how a pitfall may be incidental to the execution of a long-range plan.

We observed in Diagram 23 that a player may actually walk into a pitfall not so much out of greed as through following a principle which needs modifying. This is also true of traps, where a player ruins his game by blindly following a generally useful principle without examining the specific details of the position.

Haste, resulting in carelessness, is the bugbear of all chessplayers. Unforeseen tactical features crop up, and the player who is intent on carrying out far-reaching positional aims, will often miss a rather obvious tactical fine point. Here is how the great Capablanca went wrong in a tournament game played at Carlsbad in 1929:

(*See Diagram 34.*)

CAPABLANCA

Diagram 34 (*Black to play*)

SAEMISCH

To show you Capablanca's incredible blunder without supplying the background for his next move, would deprive this example of most of its force. Let us then examine the position in some detail:

White's doubled Queen Bishop Pawns are a strategical weakness: the Pawn on his QB4 square is hard to defend because it cannot be guarded by Pawns. It must therefore be protected by pieces—always a costly policy. Thus White is condemned to the defensive and must cede Black the initiative.

Black has several promising procedures. He can castle and then continue with . . . N—QR4 and . . . B—R3, bringing troublesome pressure to bear on the White Queen Bishop Pawn on the QB4 square. Or Black can even play . . . N—QR4 at once.

However, the safest course, as an experienced player like Capablanca well knows, is to castle first. In this way, Black avoids any unpleasant tactical possibilities stemming from White's Q—R4. Instead, Capablanca blunders with:

$$1 \ldots \ldots \qquad \text{B—R3??}$$

Acting on the admirable principle that weak Pawns should be attacked, Capablanca forgets the vital principle that one should not commence middle-game maneuvers until the King has been removed to a place of safety.

2 **Q—R4!**   . . . .

Here we have the violent move which is characteristic of a trap.

CAPABLANCA

Diagram 35 (*Black to play*)

SAEMISCH

To his dismay, Black finds that he has no less than three threats to cope with:

(a) 3 **QxB**

(b) 3 **QxNch**

(c) 3 **P—Q5**

The upshot is that no matter how Black plays, he must lose a piece. How could Capablanca have overlooked such a menacing move? He explained after the game that he saw 2 **Q—R4!** but through a mental lapse was under the impression that he could reply 2 . . . **N—QR4**—forgetting that his Queen Knight was pinned—or rather, forgetting that he had failed to castle!

Play continued:

2	**B—N2**
3 **P—Q5**	. . . .

White wins a piece and will eventually win the game because of this sizable material advantage.

Innumerable games have been lost in this way. Black has a clear positional advantage and the initiative. A little routine caution will maintain his advantage for the rest of the game. Yet one careless move gives the play a turbulent, irrelevant course that nullifies his advantage and leaves him with a fatal material minus.

Strangely enough, Capablanca committed the same mistake a few years later in the Hastings Christmas Tournament of 1934–1935—the mistake of entering upon middle-game complications before castling. Here is the position in which Capablanca went astray.

CAPABLANCA

Diagram 36 (*Black to play*)

LILIENTHAL

By playing 1 . . . N/Q2xP, Black maintains equality, keeps the King file closed and prepares to castle. But Capablanca sees an opportunity for a "clever" move, forgetting that his uncastled position has a sign clearly marked DANGER.

1 . . . .   QxKP??

Walking into a pitfall which he can hardly be blamed for overlooking. White's Queen is attacked and 2 QxQ seems forced.

2 PxN!!   . . . .

This move, which at first sight looks like a blunder, carries a powerful psychological impact.

Black has little choice in this disagreeable situation. If 2 . . .

CAPABLANCA

Diagram 37 (*Black to play*)

LILIENTHAL

QxB; 3 PxP, KR—N1; 4 P—B6!, NxP; 5 Q—B5, K—K2; 6 QR—K1 and Black is lost, as his King cannot survive on the open lines. (*6 Q—K5ch* is another winning method here.)

2		QxQ
3 PxP		. . . .

If now 3 . . . QxN; 4 PxR(Q)*ch*, N—B1 and White brings a Rook to K1 pinning the Black Queen. This variation gives you the key to the basic idea of the pitfall: White wins through his attack on the open King file against Black's uncastled King.

3		KR—N1
4 N—Q4!		. . . .

One of the most remarkable positions ever seen on the chessboard. With a Queen for only a Bishop, Black is unable to save himself! Again the explanation lies in the attack on the open King file against Black's uncastled King.

Black has no good move in this tragicomic position, for example 4 . . . Q—N7; 5 QR—K1*ch*, N—K4; 6 RxN*ch*, K—Q2; 7 R—Q5*ch*, K—K1; 8 R—K1*ch* forcing mate.

Equally interesting is 4 . . . QxQBP; 5 QR—K1*ch*, N—K4; 6 RxN*ch*, K—Q2; 7 R—K7*ch*, K—Q3; 8 N—N5*ch* forking the Queen and coming out two pieces ahead!

CAPABLANCA

Diagram 38 (*Black to play*)

LILIENTHAL

| 4 .... | Q—K5 |

A desperate attempt to neutralize the devastating attack on the King file.

| 5 QR—K1 | N—B4 |

Even worse is 5 . . . QxR; 6 RxQch, N—K4; 7 RxNch, K—Q2 —for then White picks up the King Bishop Pawn with 8 R—K7ch, whereupon his passed Pawns march down victoriously.

| 6 RxQch | NxR |
| 7 R—K1 | .... |

Winning more material on the mighty open file.

| 7 .... | RxP |
| 8 RxNch | Resigns |

With only a Rook for Bishop and Knight, Black is at a hopeless material disadvantage. Worse yet, he finds himself in a positional strait jacket after 8 . . . K—Q2; 9 P—B6, R—R2; 10 R—K7ch or 8 . . . K—B1; 9 B—K7ch, K—N1; 10 B—B6, R—R2; 11 N—B6 etc.

To appreciate the subtlety of White's pitfall, we must return to Diagram 36, where White has just captured Black's King

Pawn with a Queen Pawn which was on Q4. Thereby White set his pitfall, giving Black the choice of maintaining a playable position with . . . N/Q2xP or running into a dead lost game with . . . QxKP??

Perhaps because Capablanca was so famous a master, his occasional blunders have received more than their share of attention. In his very first international tournament (at San Sebastian, in 1911) he fell a victim to a pitfall which topped his own pitfall. It come about from the following position:

CAPABLANCA

Diagram 39 (*Black to play*)

RUBINSTEIN

White has just captured a Knight on Black's KB3 square. Black cannot very well play 1 . . . RxB, for then 2 NxP! wins material (if 2 . . . PxN; 3 BxR, QxB; 4 QxPch and 5 QxB, with the Exchange ahead. Or 2 . . . QxN; 3 QxQ, PxQ; 4 BxR with the same result).

But Black thinks he can refute the intended combination with:

1 . . . .   **QxB**

Foreseeing White's next move, Black sets a clever pitfall without realizing that he is falling into a better one.

2 NxP!!   . . . .

This is the crucial point of the pitfall. If 2 . . . PxN; 2 QxPch, K—R1; 3 BxR and White has an easy win.

Nor does 2 . . . BxPch improve matters, for then 3 K—N2, Q—R3; 4 N—B4! wins more material for White.

So far it looks as if Rubinstein has appraised the position accurately and Capablanca has no resource. What then is the nature of Black's pitfall?

CAPABLANCA

Diagram 40 (*Black to play*)

RUBINSTEIN

2	Q—R3!

This is Capablanca's pitfall. He removes the Black Queen from attack, menaces White's Bishop, and threatens to pin White's rash Knight. At first sight it seems that White can save both his attacked pieces with 3 N—B4, but Black has 3 . . . RxN!; 4 PxR, QxB in reply.

Now we begin to wonder about the soundness of White's play.

3 K—N2!	. . . .

This holds the position—at least for the time being—as . . . PxN is not yet a real threat.

3 . . . .   **QR—Q1!**

Now we see the position Capablanca had in mind when he played 1 . . . QxB. Black has moved out of the pin on his King Pawn and has pinned the Knight, with the apparently irresistible threats of . . . RxN and . . . PxN.

All this has been brilliantly calculated by Capablanca. It would seem that the pinned Knight has no escape, and that White has overreached himself. But now Rubinstein reveals the winning finesse in his plan. The move is as simple as it is logical, but only a great master could have foreseen it and its consequences.

CAPABLANCA

Diagram 41
(*White to play*)

RUBINSTEIN

4 **Q—B1!!**   . . . .

This magnificent move has several advantageous features.
First point: White's Knight is unpinned.
Second point: Black's Bishop is attacked.
Third point: if 3 . . . RxN?; 4 QxQ, PxQ; 5 BxPch winning Black's Rook on Q4 and coming out the Exchange ahead!
Fourth point: if 3 . . . QxQ; 4 BxPch followed by 5 QRxQ with two Pawns up.

4 . . . .   **PxN**

His best move under the circumstances.

5 **QxB**   . . . .

White has refuted Black's trappy play, and is at last a clear Pawn ahead. This tricky sequence is a sermon on the dangers of setting up a pitfall when you have too many vulnerable points and loose pieces of your own. Black's Bishop was wholly unprotected, his Queen Rook was only partially protected, his King Pawn was shaky, and his Queen was overburdened with attacking and defensive assignments.

Black failed, and he deserved to fail. When you set pitfalls in sound positions (as in Diagram 33), you gain in some way whether your opponent succumbs or escapes. When you set pitfalls in positions where your own weaknesses subject you to sharp retaliation (as in Diagram 39), the pitfall becomes too much of a gamble to have a likelihood of success.

PART TWO

TRAPS AND PITFALLS

IN THE OPENING

LIKE most masters, Rudolf Charousek, a famous master of the '90s, gave great thought and study to the openings. While still a youngster he copied out by hand all the analysis in Bilguer's Handbuch—a German handful which contains over a thousand pages and weighs several pounds.

Two World Champions, Lasker and Capablanca, went to the other extreme. They studied the openings as little as possible, on the theory that opening variations are as ephemeral as ladies' fashions. Their successor, Alekhine, studied the openings intensively, but always with a view to finding superficially weird-looking surprise moves, rehabilitating old discredited variations, and refuting the blindly accepted current lines.

If we went through the list of masters, we should wind up with the observation that opening play is extraordinarily personalized. Each player's opening style and preferences reflect his personality. All this variety makes opening play a colorful and confusing process quite different from the bloodless and impeccable opening lines prescribed by treatises on opening theory.

Through all this variety runs one connecting thread, the typical quality of the mistakes committed in the opening. Take a thousand games which contain opening mistakes, and with a little patience you can reduce them to a relatively small number of types.

This brings us to the question: how are these mistakes punished? Often, to be sure, the punishment is long drawn out; but in many cases, the penalty is swift and drastic, and even standardized! Traps and pitfalls in the opening are hardy perennials, because opening mistakes are perennial. In this section we shall deal with those most frequently made; and show how they are punished.

CHAPTER 4

"Transparent" Traps and Pitfalls

Some chess gimmicks are so obvious in their intent and so simple in their mechanics that you wonder that any player could be taken in by them. Carelessness, inattention, hallucination, absentmindedness—these are all possibilities. A player may be thinking of a pretty girl, of last night's television programs, or this morning's breakfast, when suddenly he finds that he has lost his Queen or been checkmated! But no matter how much we speculate, the element of wonderment remains.

How, for example, could this simple pitfall in the Budapest Defense turn up in chess magazines all over the world:

1	P—Q4	N—KB3
2	P—QB4	P—K4
3	PxP	N—N5
4	B—B4	B—N5ch
5	N—Q2	N—QB3
6	KN—B3	Q—K2
7	P—QR3	KNxKP

What now?—an oversight?

White has achieved an exemplary development, and need only continue with 8 NxN, NxN; 9 P—K3 to maintain an excellent position. Instead, he leaves his poor King in the lurch with:

(*See Diagram 42.*)

Diagram 42
(*White to play*)

8 PxB???   N—Q6 mate!

A novel smothered mate.

Now you may excuse White's falling into this naive pitfall on the ground that the Budapest Defense is a relatively new opening and its intricacies have not been fully mastered by most players. The same explanation could hardly be offered for the familiar Dragon Variation of the Sicilian Defense:

1 P—K4	P—QB4
2 N—KB3	P—Q3
3 P—Q4	PxP
4 NxP	N—KB3
5 N—QB3	N—B3
6 B—K2	P—KN3
7 B—K3	B—N2

Black hopes to simplify with 8 . . . N—KN5. But White calmly allows him to carry out the "threat."

8 Castles   N—KN5?

This costs a piece. It is a simple matter of counting.

Black expects 9 NxN (attacking the Queen), NxB (ditto); 10 NxQ, NxQ and material remains even.

9 BxN!   . . . .

Diagram 43
(*White to play*)

If now 9 . . . NxN; 10 BxB and Black is a piece down whether he captures White's Bishop or retreats his attacked Knight.

Or 9 . . . BxN; 10 B/N4xB, BxN; 11 BxNP when Black has two pieces attacked and must lose one of them!

Instead, White chooses a move which is obvious—though its consequences are not so obvious.

9 . . . .   BxB

Black may even have seen this far: if 10 QxB, NxN and Black has lost no material. But again White finds the best:

10 NxN!   . . . .

Counterattack on the Black Queen. Now Black remains a piece down whether he plays 10 . . . PxN; 11 QxB or 10 . . . BxQ; 11 NxQ. Count up the pieces in either line and you will find that Black has lost a piece!

No less surprising is the frequency with which double attacks are overlooked. An old-time favorite from the Queen's Gambit Declined starts with these moves:

1 P—Q4	P—Q4
2 P—QB4	P—QB3
3 N—KB3	N—B3
4 P—K3	P—K3

	5 N—B3	QN—Q2
	6 B—Q3	B—Q3
	7 Castles	Castles
	8 P—K4	PxKP
	9 NxP	NxN
	10 BxN	P—K4?

One of those moves that are strategically impeccable and tactically wrong. In his haste to open a diagonal for developing his Queen Bishop, Black walks into a trap that will cost him a Pawn.

Diagram 44
(*White to play*)

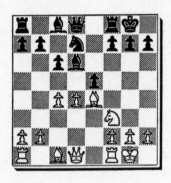

After his last move, Black is laid low by a simple double-attack mechanism.

	11 PxP	NxP
	12 NxN	BxN
	13 BxP*ch!*	. . . .

The move Black missed. His Bishop is vulnerable at K4.

	13	KxB
	14 Q—R5*ch*	K—N1
	15 QxB	. . . .

White has won a Pawn.

Nor is this an isolated instance. The development of Black's

Queen Bishop gives trouble in many openings, and is often the occasion for neat traps. Here is one from the French Defense:

1 P—K4	P—K3
2 P—Q4	P—Q4
3 N—QB3	PxP
4 NxP	N—Q2
5 N—KB3	KN—B3
6 NxNch	NxN
7 B—Q3	B—K2

Black's position is rather cramped, while White's development is free and easy.

8 Q—K2	Castles
9 B—KN5	P—QN3?

Diagram 45
(*White to play*)

White's 10 Q—K2 was a developing move, and Black took it at face value. But the Queen move was more than that—it was the prelude to a pitfall, and Black missed the point. In his eagerness to develop his Queen Bishop, he has made the same mistake as in Diagram 44; but here the error is more expensive.

10 BxN!	BxB
11 Q—K4!	. . . .

With this double attack, threatening QxRP mate and also attacking Black's Queen Rook, White forces the win of a Rook.

A cousin of the double attack with mate threat is the double attack with check. One of the most frequent examples of this device occurs in the Max Lange Attack, a tricky line recommended only to the hardiest spirits. Few openings are more exacting in the demands they make on the defender's resourcefulness.

1	P—K4	P—K4
2	N—KB3	N—QB3
3	B—B4	N—B3
4	P—Q4	PxP
5	Castles	B—B4

Black gets a more comfortable game with 5 . . . NxP; 6 R—K1, P—Q4; 7 BxP, QxB; 8 N—B3 (note the double pin!), Q—QR4; 9 NxN, B—K3 etc.

6	P—K5	P—Q4
7	PxN	PxB
8	R—K1*ch*	B—K3
9	N—N5	. . . .

An insidious pitfall, for 9 . . . QxP? seems a most natural protection for the Bishop.

Diagram 46 (*Black to play*)

9 . . . .   QxP?

The right way to guard the attacked Bishop is 9 . . . Q—Q4.

In playing the text, Black overlooks that while guarding one Bishop he is placing *the other Bishop* in jeopardy!

10	NxB	PxN
11	Q—R5*ch*	. . . .

And there we have it: double attack with check.

11	. . . .	Q—B2

A despairing swindle. Perhaps White will interpolate 12 RxP*ch*? (Black's Queen is pinned), allowing the menaced Bishop to find a safe haven by 12 . . . B—K2.

12	QxB	. . . .

He ignores the swindle and remains with a piece for two Pawns.

An amusing variant of this theme of double attack with check was current many decades ago when Steinitz's treatment of the Ruy Lopez was popular. Known as Mortimer's Trap, it went this way:

1	P—K4	P—K4
2	N—KB3	N—QB3
3	B—N5	N—B3
4	P—Q3	. . . .

Steinitz's move, with which he scored many spectacular successes during his long reign as World Champion. Nowadays the standard reply is 4 . . . P—Q3, but the pitfall we have in mind started with:

4	. . . .	N—K2

This time-wasting retreat of the Knight to an inferior square blocks the development of the King Bishop and thus offers no apparent compensation for the loss of the King Pawn. Yet it is a matter of record that this pitfall had a vogue for many years.

5 NxP?   . . . .

The artificial retreat of the Knight does not seem to arouse any suspicions in him.

Diagram 47 (*Black to play*)

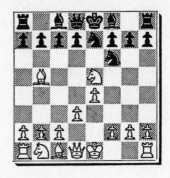

5 . . . .   **P—B3!**

This is the point of Black's heavy-handed stratagem. If the menaced Bishop retreats, Black follows up with 6 . . . **Q—R4ch** winning the Knight which is out on a limb. Now that White at last takes in the situation, he tries a swindle.

6 N—B4!?   . . . .

So that if 6 . . . **PxB???**; 7 **N—Q6 mate!** (Remember the play from Diagram 42?) But Black is prudent; his prey cannot escape.

6 . . . .   **N—N3**
7 B—R4   **P—N4**

Winning the piece after all. A simple Pawn fork does the job instead of the double attack with check.

Another transparent motif which used to take a heavy toll of victims was the offer of a piece to open the King Rook file against a castled King. Here is a plausible version from the Giuoco Piano:

1 P—K4	P—K4
2 N—KB3	N—QB3
3 B—B4	B—B4
4 P—Q3	N—B3
5 N—B3	Castles
6 B—KN5	P—KR3
7 P—KR4!?	. . . .

Diagram 48 (*Black to play*)

In leaving the attacked Bishop at his post, White offers that piece as bait to get the open King Rook file as an avenue of attack against Black's castled King. Since his intentions are transparent, we can only assume that Black underestimates the virulence of the coming attack.

7	PxB?
8 PxP	N—KN5
9 P—N6!	. . . .

Ignoring Black's counterattack and setting up a pinning attack which wins for him.

9	NxP
10 NxP!!	. . . .

With all sorts of sacrifices in mind. In the event of 10 . . . NxN he forces mate beginning with 11 R—R8ch! etc. (the perfect illustration of what he had in mind when he set up his pitfall on move 7).

And *10 . . . NxR* allows a picture mate: *11 Q—R5, R—K1; 12 PxPch, K—B1; 13 N—N6 mate!*

| 10 . . . . | NxQ |

White's attack is so powerful that even without his Queen he can carry out a sinister King-hunt:

11 PxPch	RxP
12 BxRch	K—B1
13 R—R8ch	K—K2
14 N—Q5ch	K—Q3
15 N—QB4 mate!	

This pitfall *may* not stand up under the most searching analysis; but in any event we cannot help wondering at the fool-hardiness of any player who would subject himself to such a cascade of sacrifices without having the defensive skill to resist the assault.

In all the examples in this chapter we have played over pitfalls where the attacker's objectives were quite obvious or would become so after a little study. As for the trap in Diagram 44, Black's loss of a Pawn does not seem too difficult to foresee. Yet some of these traps and pitfalls have had many victims over the years. Forewarned is forearmed!

CHAPTER 5

The Harried King

In the sixteenth century chess competition was still in such a rudimentary stage that Bishop Ruy Lopez, one of the best players of the time, advised his readers to place the board so that the light would shine in their opponent's eyes. Chess tactics were not much further advanced, for the chief theme of pitfalls and other attacks was to concentrate on the King's weak point, the KB2 square.

Nowadays, when we enjoy such a variety of attacking ideas and methods, the attack on KB7 receives much less emphasis. At the turn of the century no chess primer was complete without a sober warning about the perils of the Scholar's Mate:

1	P–K4	P–K4
2	B–B4	. . . .

It was not until about 1830 that this move gave way to 2 N–KB3 as the popular continuation. The aim of the Bishop move is of course to hit at KB7.

2	. . . .	B–B4
3	Q–R5	. . . .

Threatening 4 QxKP*ch* and above all 4 QxBP **mate.**

3	. . . .	N–QB3???

He sees the minor threat but not the major one.

4 QxBP mate

Diagram 49

SCHOLAR'S MATE!

While we are not likely to see the Scholar's Mate often today, the motif of attack against KB7 is still a useful one, especially against inexperienced players. In its modern form, the theme appears in a variety of guises and it is not always easy for the prospective victim to see the dangers in store for him. In the following example from the Center Game, the finish is astonishingly abrupt:

1	P—K4	P—K4
2	P—Q4	PxP
3	QxP	N—QB3
4	Q—K3	N—B3
5	B—B4	. . . .

White is unlucky in his choice of moves. The premature Queen moves lose time, and so does the development of the Bishop.

5	. . . .	N—K4
6	B—N3	B—N5*ch*

The vague outlines of a pitfall begin to shape up. White would do well to develop with 7 N—QB3 or 7 B—Q2, instead of weakening his position with:

7 P—QB3?   B—B4!

This is ominous; if 8 QxB??, N—Q6ch forks White's King and Queen.

The "best" retreat is 8 Q—K2, though it leaves Black with a sizable lead in development and consequently much the better game. This gives White the suicidal idea of playing an "aggressive" move:

8 Q—N3??   . . . .

Diagram 50 (*Black to play*)

8 . . . .   **BxPch!!**
Resigns

One of the most captivating pitfalls ever devised on the chessboard. If 9 QxB, N—Q6ch, forking King and Queen. Or 9 KxB, NxPch, forking King and Queen just the same. Three possible royal forks in an eight-move game! Very ingenious.

The theme of attack against KB7 appears in many variations of Philidor's Defense. What seems to be only a slight inexactitude on Black's part may expose him to serious loss of material.

1 P—K4   P—K4
2 N—KB3   P—Q3

3 P—Q4	N—Q2
4 B—QB4	. . . .

This natural developing move involves many pitfalls unless Black plays with great care. His proper course now is 4 . . . P—QB3, keeping White's Queen out of Q5. Is that important? Study the following play!

4	KN—B3?

One of the rare cases where this excellent developing move is a mistake.

Diagram 51
(*White to play*)

5 PxP	. . . .

Now Black realizes that he has stumbled into a pitfall. The instinctive reply 5 . . . PxP?? is refuted by 6 N—N5 with an attack on Black's King Bishop Pawn that cannot be parried.

Another variation on the same theme: if 5 . . . KNxP?; 6 Q—Q5 winning the venturesome Knight because of the threatened 7 QxBP mate.

5	QNxP
6 NxN	PxN
7 BxPch	. . . .

White has had his way after all. Black now indulges in some mild fireworks, which still leave him a Pawn down.

7	KxB!?
8 QxQ	B—QN5*ch*
9 Q—Q2	BxQ*ch*
10 NxB	. . . .

White's material advantage should win for him.

The same concluding comment applies to the related Philidor variation which begins:

1 P—K4	P—K4
2 N—KB3	P—Q3
3 P—Q4	N—Q2
4 B—QB4	B—K2?

As we have seen, the safe move is 4 . . . P—QB3.

Diagram 52
(*White to play*)

Black is already in a pitfall, and his dubious "best" is the loss of a Pawn.

5 PxP	. . . .

If now 5 . . . NxP; 6 NxN, PxN; 7 Q—R5 (again stressing the attack against KB7) winning the King Pawn in reply to Black's virtually forced 7 . . . P—KN3.

5	PxP?

6 **Q—Q5**   . . . .

Still hammering away at the same idea.

6	. . . .	**N—N3**
7	**QxBP**ch	**K—Q2**
8	**NxP**ch	**K—Q3**

White can now win as he pleases—say 9 **P—B4** or 9 **B—B4**.

Another pitfall which illustrates the same theme turns up as early as the second move of the King's Gambit Declined:

1	**P—K4**	**P—K4**
2	**P—KB4**	**B—B4**

Diagram 53
(*White to play*)

The usual reply is 3 **N—KB3** (sound development). To capture the King Pawn would be a crass blunder inviting immediate retaliation:

3 **PxP??**   **Q—R5**ch

White is lost! He has the grim choice between 4 **K—K2, QxKP** mate or 4 **P—KN3, QxKP**ch and Black wins the King Rook (double attack with check).

The play from Diagram 53 shows the dangers of an early advance of the King Bishop Pawn in openings where both players have played P—K4. This is especially true of Black's playing . . . P—KB3. Here is a trap from the King's Knight's Gambit that makes the point impressively:

1	P—K4	P—K4
2	P—KB4	PxP
3	N—KB3	P—KN4
4	B—B4	P—KB3?

Though this move looks solid, it really leaves the Black King's defenses in a flimsy state. (The developing move *4 . . . B—N2* has been standard for centuries.)

Diagram 54
(*White to play*)

Having played only Pawn moves, Black is in no condition to resist a brisk assault.

5	NxP!	PxN
6	Q—R5*ch*	. . . .

This deadly stroke was made possible by *4 . . . P—KB3?*

6	. . . .	K—K2
7	Q—B7*ch*	K—Q3
8	Q—Q5*ch*	K—K2
9	Q—K5 mate	

The mating position reminds us of a variation in the previous example.

The removal of the King Bishop Pawn can also prove dangerous in other openings as well, as you can see from this Caro-Kann pitfall:

	1	P—K4	P—QB3
	2	P—Q4	P—Q4
	3	B—Q3	. . . .

An inferior move which Black can answer effectively with 3 . . . PxP; 4 BxP, N—B3 seizing the initiative.

| | 3 | . . . . | N—B3? |

This is development of a sort, but singularly ill timed.

| | 4 | P—K5 | KN—Q2 |
| | 5 | P—K6! | . . . . |

Setting the pitfall.

Diagram 55 (*Black to play*)

This pitfall, like some earlier examples, is incidental to a long-range plan. If Black succumbs, he is mated in spectacular fashion; if he sees through the pitfall, he is nevertheless burdened with lasting positional disadvantages. Whatever Black's reaction may be, White stands to gain.

Comparatively best for Black is 5 . . . N—B3; 6 PxPch, KxP. In that event, Black cannot castle, his King Pawn is backward, his development slow and unpromising. But he would still have a game to play—which is not the case after:

5	PxP???

Overlooking the pitfall.

6 Q—R5ch	P—KN3
7 QxNPch!	. . . .

7 BxPch achieves the same result, but the Queen capture is prettier.

7	PxQ
8 BxP mate!	

The triumph of mind over matter.

So far we have been studying the storming of the vulnerable point KB7 by means of combined Queen-and-Bishop attacks. But Queen-and-Knight attacks are equally formidable, as Horowitz proved in a famous gamelet played during the Prague International Team Tournament of 1931. This pitfall also turned up in a Caro-Kann:

1 P—K4	P—QB3
2 P—Q4	P—Q4
3 N—QB3	PxP
4 NxP	B—B4
5 N—N3	B—N3
6 P—KR4	P—KR3
7 N—KB3	P—K3?

An inexactitude. 7 . . . N—Q2! is safer.

	8 N—K5!	B—R2
	9 B—QB4	N—Q2
	10 Q—K2	....

White's last move was played to avoid the exchange of Queens after . . . NxN. But 10 Q—K2 is more versatile than it looks—it sets a pitfall.

	10	KN—B3??

He suspects nothing. 10 . . . NxN was essential.

GUDJU

Diagram 56
(*White to play*)

HOROWITZ

	11 NxKBP!	....

This was the incidental point of White's last move. If 11 . . . KxN; 12 QxPch, K—N3; 13 P—R5 mate!

	11	B—N5*ch*

A "spite check."

	12 P—QB3	Resigns

As Black cannot capture the intruder, the cost of playing on would be to move his Queen and lose a whole Rook. So Black surrenders.

To dwell overmuch on the weakness of the square KB2 might give us an altogether disquieting impression. In all the examples we have seen in this chapter, the victim of a trap or pitfall comes to grief because he neglects his development and thus makes a pitfall possible. A pronounced weakness at KB2 is therefore a special case of inept development, which can take many other forms. What these are, and how they can be exploited, will be the subject of the next chapter.

CHAPTER 6

Inept Development

Perhaps you are familiar with Znosko-Borovsky's observation, in his classic work *The Middle Game in Chess,* that a player may be ahead in time, space, and force—and yet be summarily checkmated!

Paul Morphy, the greatest player of his day, owed his successes to his flair for quick development. Wilhelm Steinitz, the greatest player of *his* day, had a taste for slow development. In some of his games he postponed castling to the 20th move or so; in one of his most celebrated masterpieces* he made five moves in the opening with a Knight. (This included returning the Knight to its original square.) Frank Marshall once won a sprightly game in which his first fourteen moves were *all Pawn moves!*

The Viennese master, Ernst Gruenfeld, has the reputation of knowing more about the openings than any other player. From this encyclopedic knowledge he has distilled the uninspiring conviction that every game should be a draw. Tchigorin, a great attacking player of the past and also a noted opening authority, was of the opinion that he could always win with the White pieces by playing 1 P—K4. To this he added the corollary that he could always win with the Black pieces by answering 1 P—K4 with 1 . . . P—K4.

To make confusion thrice confounded, the Hungarian Breyer claimed that in the opening position (with all the pieces and

* Against Anderssen (Vienna, 1873).

Pawns still unmoved), White's game was in the last throes. Compare this with Tartakover's cynical dictum that any opening is good enough to be played if its reputation is bad enough. In one of Alekhine's most famous games, his opponent had two Queens shortly after the opening was over—but Alekhine had three, and checkmated him neatly!

One thing is clear—despite all attempts to reduce opening play to rigid analyses, there is enormous scope for individual taste and aberration. Though the opening authorities dwell in a bedlam of raucous disagreement, their very differences help to make chess the lively game it is. And, so long as the element of the incalculable and the unforeseen exists in the chess openings, just so long will traps and pitfalls flourish in the early part of the game.

As long as there are players who develop their pieces with less than maximum efficiency, inept development will be the chief contributing cause of traps and pitfalls. These gimmicks are at their deadliest when the intended victim has brought out his forces awkwardly. Communication is bad, cooperation is conspicuous by its absence; and an alert, tactically minded opponent will soon see a chance for a pitfall.

One of the most effective ways to exploit the difficulties of awkwardly posted pieces is to pin them. That is why you will find many examples of pins in the pitfalls that make up this chapter. One of the best known turns up in the familiar Tarrasch Trap in the Ruy Lopez:

1	P—K4	P—K4
2	N—KB3	N—QB3
3	B—N5	P—QR3
4	B—R4	N—B3
5	Castles	NxP
6	P—Q4	P—QN4
7	B—N3	P—Q4
8	PxP	B—K3
9	P—B3	B—K2
10	R—K1	Castles
11	N—Q4!?	. . . .

Diagram 57 (*Black to play*)

Despite the comfortable appearance of Black's development, it has a flaw resulting from the early advance 6 . . . P—QN4. Black's Queen Knight has no Pawn protection.

White's 11 N—Q4!? peremptorily highlights this difficulty. The move is a promising prelude to a pitfall, for it gives Black a bewildering choice of alternatives. And bewilderment leads to doubt, uncertainty, hesitancy, timidity—even panic.

What are Black's choices in Diagram 57? If he takes the "simplest" course (11 . . . NxN; 12 PxN), he is left with a backward Pawn on the newly opened Queen Bishop file and his advanced Knight threatens to go lost by 13 P—B3, N—N4; 14 P—KR4. We cannot blame Black for finding this line distasteful.

Now back to Diagram 57. Black has a complicated alternative in 11 . . . NxKP!? But then White has a pin on the King file which he can exploit with 12 P—B3 winning a piece. However, after 12 . . . B—Q3; 13 PxN, B—KN5 (followed by . . . Q—R5) Black gets a menacing attack which may well be worth the piece sacrificed. If Black's counterattack proved successful, we would have to dismiss 11 N—Q4!? as a faulty pitfall. But whereas Black found 11 . . . NxN too passive, he finds 11 . . . NxKP!? too speculative.

So again we return to Diagram 57. Black seeks the "golden mean," and thinks he has found it in:

11 . . . .   Q—Q2?

Guarding the unprotected Knight, Black will find that he has left his other Knight in the lurch!

Diagram 58
(*White to play*)

12 **NxB!**   . . . .

This unexpected move wins a piece. If 12 . . . QxN; 13 RxN!, PxR??; 14 BxQ. Or 12 . . . PxN; 13 RxN!, PxR??; 14 QxQ. The fact that Black's Queen Pawn is pinned on the diagonal and on the file as well, emphasizes the flaw in Black's development.

A useful principle suggested by this pitfall is that the more choices you give your opponent, the more likely he is to be taken in by a pitfall. In the following example from the Queen's Indian Defense we see this principle at work:

1	P—Q4	N—KB3
2	P—QB4	P—K3
3	N—KB3	P—QN3
4	B—N5	B—N2
5	P—K3	P—KR3!

A sly preparation for the coming pitfall. White is not yet in danger, but he must have his wits about him.

6 **B—R4**   **B—N5ch**

Setting the pitfall. The wrong reply will cost White a piece.

Diagram 59
(*White to play*)

If White plays 7 **N—B3** or 7 **KN—Q2**, he comes off unscathed. But he makes the wrong choice, and loses a piece.

7 **QN—Q2?**   . . . .

Wrongly relying on general principles. He avoids 7 **KN—Q2**, for that would mean moving the same piece twice in the opening. And he dismisses 7 **N—B3**, for that might lead to doubled Pawns—a likely positional weakness. As in Diagram 34, he goes wrong by slavish adherence to general principles.

7 . . . .   **P—KN4!**
8 **B—N3**   **P—N5!**

Now White realizes that he has been gulled. His attacked Knight cannot budge from KB3, for then 9 . . . **N—K5** wins the pinned Knight. (Now we see the importance of 5 . . . **P—KR3!**, partly as a preparation for unpinning Black's King Knight, partly as a preparation for 7 . . . **P—KN4!** and 8 . . . **P—N5!**)

9 **P—QR3**   . . . .

A swindle. If Black heedlessly plays 9 . . . **BxNch?**, White retakes with his menaced Knight, and the pitfall disappears.

On the other hand, if Black plays 9 . . . **PxN** he loses his pinning Bishop. And if he tries 9 . . . B—R4, he has to reckon with *10* P—N4. Must we conclude that White has escaped from the pitfall?

Diagram 60 (*Black to play*)

9	PxN!

The pitfall works after all! Black has a winning Pawn fork in reserve.

10 PxB	PxP

The charming point of the pitfall. The Pawn fork, supported at long range by the fianchettoed Bishop, wins a piece after all.

11 BxNP	BxB *

Another surprising Pawn fork proves equally effective in the Giuoco Piano, a deceptively placid opening that is rich in gimmicks. Here are the introductory moves:

1 P—K4	P—K4
2 N—KB3	N—QB3

---

* Black has an easy win with his extra piece. As an amusing "human interest" touch, it should be mentioned that Black, a master of the first rank, blundered later on and lost the game! (Tarrasch-Bogolyubov, Gothenburg, 1920.)

3	B—B4	B—B4
4	P—Q3	N—B3
5	N—B3	P—Q3
6	B—KN5	P—KR3
7	BxN	QxB
8	N—Q5	Q—Q1
9	P—B3	. . . .

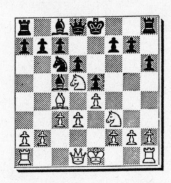

Diagram 61 (*Black to play*)

White's last move sets up a pitfall that is all the more insidious for looking quite harmless. Once more the opponent has a multiple choice. Black can play 9 . . . Castles or 9 . . . B—KN5 or 9 . . . B—K3 or 9 . . . N—K2 or even 9 . . . N—R4. (In reply to 9 . . . N—R4 Black need not fear the Pawn fork 10 P—QN4—he has 10 . . . NxB as a way out.)

Black's multiple choice is of a different kind from the one he had in Diagram 57. There the choice was difficult because the alternatives were unpleasant in one way or another. Here the choice is burdensome because the alternatives are rather colorless. How choose among them?

Of the five alternatives open to Black in Diagram 61, four are unobjectionable, the remaining one loses. Here it is:

9	. . . .	B—K3?
10	P—Q4	. . . .

This wins a piece—despite Black's ingenious squirming. If

Black tries to avoid the later Pawn fork by 10 . . . BxN; 11
KPxB, N—R4, he loses a piece just the same after 12 PxB, NxB; 13
Q—R4ch (double attack with check).

10	PxP
11 PxP	. . . .

Here again Black can make an effort to avoid the Pawn fork
by resorting to 11 . . . BxN; 12 KPxB, B—N5ch. But after the
tricky 13 K—B1! White must win the exposed Bishop once the
attacked Knight retreats (14 Q—R4ch—again double attack with
check).

11	B—N3
12 NxB	RPxN
13 P—Q5	. . . .

Here is the Pawn fork to which Black exposed himself by playing 9 . . . B—K3? But Black still doesn't give up hope and tries
to wriggle out.

Diagram 62 (*Black to play*)

13	N—R4!

An attempted swindle which nearly comes off. The idea is that
after 14 PxB? (hasty!), NxB, Black has avoided loss of material,
as White is unable to play 15 Q—R4ch with Black's Queen Rook
trained on that square. But White has the last laugh with:

14 B—Q3!	B—N5

The pitfall ends with White's win of a piece—the attacked Knight has no retreat. A delightful battle of wits!

In the previous trap White's Pawns played starring roles. Black's Pawns are no less important in that ancient stratagem known as the Noah's Ark Trap. There are several versions of this Ruy Lopez pitfall, the best-known one starting with these moves:

1	P—K4	P—K4
2	N—KB3	N—QB3
3	B—N5	P—QR3
4	B—R4	N—B3
5	N—B3	P—Q3
6	P—Q4	. . . .

Not a mistake, but it may turn out to be the prelude to one. From now on, White must be careful.

6 . . . .   P—QN4

A pitfall—and a nasty one; as far as White is concerned, it is almost a reflex action to retreat his threatened Bishop.

The fact is, though, that 7 PxP is a far wiser course, saving the Bishop from being trapped by a net of Black Pawns.

Diagram 63
(*White to play*)

7 B—N3?	NxQP!
8 NxN	PxN
9 QxP?	. . . .

Succumbing to the pitfall in its most costly form; but after some such move as 9 N—K2, Black remains a clear Pawn ahead with 9 . . . P—B4 (not 9 . . . NxP?? allowing the double attack 10 B—Q5).

9	P—B4

The avenging Pawns roll into action. No matter where White's Queen retreats, the reply 10 . . . P—B5 traps White's Bishop at QN3.

A modern offshoot of the Noah's Ark Trap makes use of the same Ruy Lopez theme:

1 P—K4	P—K4
2 N—KB3	N—QB3
3 B—N5	P—QR3
4 B—R4	P—Q3
5 P—Q4	. . . .

White has safer alternatives in 5 Castles or 5 P—B3 or 5 BxNch, PxB; 6 P—Q4.

5	P—QN4!

As in the previous example, this sets up the pitfall.

6 B—N3	NxP
7 NxN	PxN
8 QxP??	. . . .

Now he is in the pitfall, though he can struggle for survival. (8 B—Q5 is the move to save the Bishop.)

8	P—QB4
9 Q—Q5	. . . .

An attempt to swindle by attacking the unguarded Black Rook

Diagram 64 (*Black to play*)

and threatening 10 **QxBP** mate at the same time (double attack with mate threat). But Black has it all figured out.

9 . . . .   **B—K3!**

9 . . . **P—B5?** would not do because it would lose the Queen Rook.

10 **Q—B6***ch*   . . . .

Still hoping to gain time to save his threatened Bishop.

10 . . . .   **B—Q2!**

By continuing to attack the Queen, Black deprives White of the time he needs to save his Bishop.

11 **Q—Q5**   . . . .

Renewing the mating threat. But now Black can play . . . **P—B5**, *as his Rook is protected.*

11 . . . .   **P—B5**

Trapping the Bishop as planned. (*Diagram 65.*)

No less a master than the great Alekhine once overlooked this pitfall.

The fitting comment on the last few examples is, "Never underestimate the power of a Pawn." There are other pitfalls in which a "measly Pawn" proves to be the enemy's undoing. One

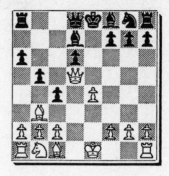

Diagram 65
(*White to play*)

of the most impressive occurs in the exceedingly trappy Cambridge Springs variation of the Queens Gambit Declined:

1	P—Q4	P—Q4
2	P—QB4	P—K3
3	N—QB3	N—KB3
4	B—N5	QN—Q2
5	P—K3	P—B3
6	N—B3	Q—R4

Black's underlying thought in this line of play is to strive for counterattack. He pins White's Queen Knight which is deprived of its natural protection by the Queen Bishop.

7 N—Q2   . . . .

This unpinning move neutralizes a possible . . . N—K5 and is therefore excellent. However, it leaves White's Bishop on KN5 unguarded. Though there is nothing wrong with White's last move, he must be careful about his coming moves.

7 . . . .   B—N5

With his last move Black has set a pitfall. As he attacks White's Knight on QB3 twice, White's most likely reply is a Queen move.

Which Queen move? Well, 8 **Q—N3?** seems to be in order. But that would mean falling into the pitfall: Black replies 8

Diagram 66
(*White to play*)

. . . **PxP!**—an innocent-looking Pawn move that attacks White's
Queen *and also opens up the rank* for an attack by Black's
Queen on White's Bishop at KN5. Here White can try a swindle: 9 **NxP**, attacking Black's Queen and hoping for 9 . . . **QxB?**,
which allows the reply 10 **QxB** and all's well.

But Black can win a piece after all—after 8 **Q—N3?, PxP!;** 9
NxP, he momentarily disregards the attack on his Queen to in-
terpolate 9 . . . **BxN CHECK.** After White recaptures, 10 . . .
QxB wins the Bishop.

This little excursion is a much-needed reminder that hair-
sharp timing is of the essence in assuring the success of many a
pitfall.

To return to Diagram 66: White sees the pitfall set for him
and plays soundly:

8 **Q—B2**   **Castles**

Just as Black had a number of colorless alternatives to choose
from in Diagram 61, so White has a choice of several character-
less moves here: 9 **B—K2** or 9 **B—Q3** or 9 **BxN.**

White dismisses 9 **B—K2** as too conservative; he fancies the
Bishop as a slightly stronger piece, hence he does not relish giving up a Bishop for a Knight by 9 **BxN.** There remains:

9 **B—Q3?**   . . . .

Falling into the pitfall this time. Either of the two alternative
moves mentioned was preferable.

Diagram 67
(*White to play*)

| 9 . . . . | **PxP!** |

Now this Pawn move wins a piece.

| 10 **BxN** | . . . . |

With both Bishops attacked, White has no choice. Perhaps his swindle will work—after 10 . . . NxB the danger will have disappeared.

| 10 . . . . | **BPxB!** |

Another Pawn move—White loses a piece, as his Queen is attacked.

| 11 **QxP** | **NxB** |

An even subtler Pawn move wins a piece for Black in an unusual variation of the Reti Opening:

1	**N—KB3**	**P—Q4**
2	**P—B4**	**PxP**
3	**N—R3**	**P—K4**
4	**NxKP**	**BxN**
5	**Q—R4ch**	**P—QN4!**

This might be called a pitfall for development.

If White pauses to capture the cocky Pawn, he never has time to take the Bishop at his QR3. For example: 6 QxNP*ch*, P—QB3;

Diagram 68
(White to play)

7 NxP/6, NxN; 8 QxNch, B—Q2; 9 Q—K4ch and now Black keeps his extra piece with 9 . . . B—K2!

| | 6 QxB | B—N2 |
| | 7 P—QN3 | Q—Q3! |

A pitfall that is incidental to Black's plan of development. If White exchanges Queens—his best course—he loses time retreating his attacked Knight. So, as Black has anticipated, White guards his Knight at K5. Against this move Black has prepared an astounding pitfall:

| | 8 B—N2? | P—B6!! |

Diagram 69
(White to play)

A position worth dwelling on. No matter how White plays, he must lose a piece—and maybe more.

Thus, if 9 PxP, QxN.

Or 9 BxP??, QxQ.

Or finally 9 QxQ, PxQ and both Knight and Bishop are attacked: White must lose a piece.

(Note, by the way, that in this last variation, Black can go wrong after 9 QxQ by playing 9 . . . PxB??. The saving clause for White in that case is 10 Q—Q4!)

Spectacular as 8 . . . P—B6!! undoubtedly is, we must remember that White's inept development gives Black his opportunity for a refutation.

Awkward or incomplete development is always a shaky basis on which to begin maneuvers that are more appropriate to the middle game. Black learns this to his cost in a variation of the French Defense:

1	P—K4	P—K3
2	P—Q4	P—Q4
3	N—QB3	B—N5
4	P—K5	P—QB4
5	P—QR3	PxP
6	QxP	N—QB3

Excellent; Black develops with gain of time by attacking the White Queen.

7	Q—N4	BxN*ch*
8	PxB	. . . .

Diagram 70 (*Black to play*)

Black has a wide choice of moves here, and one of them will lead to a pitfall with a tricky point. Two moves above all are worth considering: 8 . . . Q—B2 (so that if 9 QxNP, QxP*ch* saving the attacked Rook); or 8 . . . NxP (so that if 9 QxNP, Q—B3 likewise saving the attacked Rook). One of these moves really does the job, the other is a sham which loses at least the Exchange in unexpected fashion.

Black chooses the wrong move:

8	NxP?
9 QxNP	Q—B3

This only *appears* to save the Rook.

10 B—KR6!!	. . . .

First point: Black cannot play 10 . . . NxB??? losing his Queen, while 10 . . . QxB costs him the exchange after 11 QxR.

Second point: Black cannot play an indifferent move, for then comes 11 QxQ, NxQ; 12 B—N7 winning a piece (double attack).

Third point: 10 . . . K—K2??? will not do, for then 11 B—KN5 pins (and wins) the Black Queen.

Diagram 71 (*Black to play*)

10	N—Q2!

Black's only hope of swindling his way out. With his Queen protected, he now threatens to win a piece with 11 . . . NxB.

And, of course, after *11 QxQ?*, KNxQ his Knight on KB3 is protected, so that he has nothing to fear from *12 B—N7.*

Has White overreached himself? Not at all—

$$11 \; \text{B—QN5!} \quad \dots$$

Now all the threats are renewed. The main threats are *12 Q—B8* checkmate as well as *12 QxQ, KNxQ; 13 B—N7* winning a piece because Black's Knight at Q2 is pinned and therefore useless as a protecting piece.

What are Black's resources? He cannot play *11 . . . NxB???* for after *12 QxQ* his Queen is lost (again the pin defeats him!). Nor can Black relieve the pin with *11 . . . K—K2???* or *11 . . . K—Q1???* which allows the brutal pin *12 B—N5* winning the Queen.

Diagram 72 (*Black to play*)

There is no defense. Black must lose at least a piece.

In sharp contrast is this final example from the Two Knights' Defense, in which Black ruins his game as early as the 9th move by inept development:

1 P—K4	P—K4
2 N—KB3	N—QB3
3 B—B4	N—B3
4 P—Q4	PxP
5 Castles	P—Q3

Black is better off with *5 . . . NxP.* The move he actually plays gives him a cramped, colorless game.

6	NxP	B—K2
7	N—QB3	Castles
8	P—KR3	. . . .

Diagram 73 (*Black to play*)

In order to obtain some playing room for his pieces, Black must try to undo the effects of his mechanical development. He plans . . . N—Q2 with a view to . . . B—B3 followed by . . . N/Q2—K4. Whether this will really ease his position is doubtful; but in any event, he must be vigilant against any rapid exploitation on White's part of his ineffective development. As we see from Black's very next move, he does not take the position as seriously as he ought to.

8 . . . .   R—K1?

Played with singular lack of judgment. In the face of the strong diagonal pressure against KB7 exerted by White's Bishop on QB4, Black ought to keep the weak spot guarded by his King Rook, and proceed at once with 8 . . . N—Q2.

9 R—K1   . . . .

Now that Black has weakened his KB2, he can no longer remove his King Knight from KB3 to Q2—for that would weaken his King-side beyond endurance.

But Black is blind to the difficulties of his position, and instead of trying 9 . . . N—K4, which would at least offer temporary relief, he blunders into a fatal trap which he has constructed with his own feeble moves.

9 . . . .   N—Q2??

Diagram 74
(*White to play*)

10 BxPch!!   KxB
11 N—K6!!   KxN

On any other move, he loses his Queen.

12 Q—Q5ch   K—B3
13 Q—KB5 mate!

The loser here was Dr. Siegbert Tarrasch, who had played a match for the World Championship four years earlier! After such a loss, and by such a master, it would be anticlimactic to say any more on the subject of inept development and the dangerous traps and pitfalls to which it leads.

CHAPTER 7

_____

Greed Doesn't Pay

Frank Marshall, the great American master, staunchly upheld the view that in chess it is more blessed to give than to receive. He despised players who were always avid for material gain, and his games are studded with speculative sacrifices and gimmicks. Even on the rare occasions when Marshall was defending, he favored indirect defenses which looked like oversights. To Marshall it was second nature to set pitfalls for the materialists by temperament.

Greed has been many a player's undoing. In his concentration on material gain, he often overlooks pitfalls based on a tactical finesse. Relying on the principle that material advantage generally assures victory, he is prone to forget other principles—those that warn against neglecting the King's safety, against running into embarrassing pins, against losing valuable time, and the like.

In one of Marshall's books he tells the classic story of a poor man who had called his three sons to his deathbed. "My sons," he told them, "I have nothing in the way of worldly goods to leave you. But I have a piece of good advice for you which is worth more than gold. *Never capture the Queen Knight Pawn with your Queen!*"

This advice is certainly psychologically sound. Sometimes greed seems nature's device for seeing to it that chessplayers remain somewhat less than perfect.

The most amusing paradox about greedy play is that occasionally, instead of leading to gain of material, it leads to loss of more valuable material. This is neatly brought out in a Queen's Gambit pitfall which has proved a will-o'-the-wisp for countless players:

1 P—Q4	P—Q4
2 P—QB4	PxP
3 P—K3	P—QN4?

It has often been said that a bad plan is better than none at all. However, bad plans have led consistently and logically to defeat. In this case Black clings stubbornly to the faulty plan of holding on to the gambit Pawn.

4 P—QR4	. . . .

Now 4 . . . P—QR3 looks like the natural move to round out Black's Pawn formation on the Queen-side, but after 5 PxP Black's Queen Rook Pawn is pinned and cannot recapture.

4	P—QB3
5 PxP	PxP??

Consistent to the last—but now he loses a piece.

6 Q—B3!	. . . .

Diagram 75 (*Black to play*)

Centuries old, this pitfall still continues to bring disaster to greedy players.

Another pitfall from the same opening punishes greediness even more drastically:

1	P—Q4	P—Q4
2	P—QB4	PxP
3	N—KB3	P—QB4
4	P—K3	PxP
5	BxP	PxP??

Diagram 76
(*White to play*)

Black foolishly expects 6 QxQch, KxQ—when he will remain a Pawn ahead after 7 BxBP, PxPch or 7 BxKP, P—K3. But White's pitfall is based on an inversion in the order of the moves:

| 6 | BxBP*ch!* | KxB |
| 7 | QxQ | . . . . |

And instead of winning a Pawn, Black has lost his Queen!

In the following example from the Falkbeer Counter Gambit, White does not even have the excuse of having been misled by a transposition of moves:

1	P—K4	P—K4
2	P—KB4	P—Q4
3	N—KB3	QPxP
4	NxP	N—QB3
5	B—N5	. . . .

This pinning move threatens to win the Exchange—a threat that White carries out. How does Black defend against the threat?

5 . . . .   N—B3!

He doesn't defend at all—or rather, he defends in the manner of Marshall, by setting a pitfall.

6 NxN   PxN

7 BxPch   B—Q2

Diagram 77
(*White to play*)

The crucial position. White can remain a Pawn up after 8 BxBch, QxB in return for Black's lead in development. But White is too greedy to see that he is heading straight into a pitfall:

8 BxR??   B—KN5!

White's Queen is lost!

There are times when haste proves just as disastrous as greed. In either case, a player rushes headlong into trouble he might have avoided with a little care and patience. The moral is very effectively pointed in a Petroff Defense pitfall which is one of the best known in the whole repertoire of opening pitfalls:

1 P—K4   P—K4

2 N—KB3   N—KB3

3 NxP   . . . .

Now Black can automatically maintain the balance of power by playing 3 . . . NxP? But this automatic recapture is bad. (The right way is 3 . . . P—Q3 first. Then, after 4 N—KB3, the reply 4 . . . NxP is perfectly safe, as the pin 5 Q—K2 is met by 5 . . . Q—K2.)

| 3 . . . . | NxP? |
| 4 Q—K2! | . . . . |

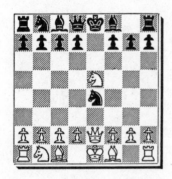

Diagram 78 (*Black to play*)

White's last move sets a nasty pitfall. The attacked Knight dare not budge: if 4 . . . N—KB3???; 5 N—B6 dis *ch* wins the Black Queen.

Having captured in haste, Black can now repent at leisure. He rightly realizes that the best way—relatively speaking—to meet White's pin is to set up a counterpin.

| 4 . . . . | Q—K2 |
| 5 QxN | P—Q3 |

The counterpin. Now it is White who cannot move his advanced Knight on pain of losing his Queen. But he can come out at least a Pawn to the good, as the following play proves.

| 6 P—Q4 | P—KB3 |

7 P—KB4	N—Q2

Black wants to regain the Knight—but not at the cost of a Pawn. This tempts him into a pitfall.

8 N—QB3!	. . . .

An excellent developing move which guards White's Queen and thus threatens to retreat White's attacked Knight. In addition, the move prepares for N—Q5, which will make it possible for White to remain a Pawn ahead.

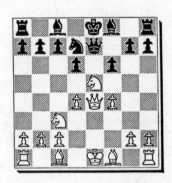

Diagram 79 (*Black to play*)

The strength of White's last move is seen in the variation 8 . . . BPxN; 9 N—Q5. Black cannot play 9 . . . Q—K3??? (because of 10 NxPch forking King and Queen). He must therefore content himself with 9 . . . Q—Q1, remaining a Pawn down after 10 BPxP etc.

8	QPxN
9 N—Q5!	. . . .

This sets a new pitfall. As in the variation just given, Black must resign himself to the loss of a Pawn by playing 9 . . . Q—Q1.

9	Q—Q3?

An ill-judged attempt to maintain material equality.

10	BPxP	PxP
11	PxP	. . . .

White's pitfall is now in good working order, and will win at least the Exchange for him.

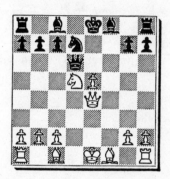

Diagram 80 (*Black to play*)

Black cannot reply *11 . . . QxP?* for then his Queen is pinned, allowing *12 NxPch* which wins at least the Exchange and may win a whole Rook.

Nor can Black play *11 . . . NxP?* because of the pin *12 B—KB4* which wins a piece at once.

11	. . . .	Q—QB3
12	B—QN5!	. . . .

Forcing Black's Queen away from her protection of the Queen Bishop Pawn (if *12 . . . QxB???; 13 NxPch* forks King and Queen).

12	. . . .	Q—KN3

The *only* move that does not lose the Queen! (If *12 . . . Q—B4; 13 B—K3* and the Queen has no flight square.)

13	QxQch	PxQ
14	NxPch	. . . .

White ends up the pitfall with an overwhelming material advantage.

An equally useful pitfall, and one which catches even more victims, is the terror of inexperienced players who know less about the Queen's Gambit Declined than they should. If ever greed seems justified, it is in this all too plausible pitfall, which calls on Black to defy the power of a pin and "lose" his Queen in the process:

1 P—Q4	P—Q4
2 P—QB4	P—K3
3 N—QB3	N—KB3
4 B—N5	QN—Q2

Unbelievable, thinks White. The game has barely started, and already Black has blundered.

Actually this "oversight" is a pitfall.

5 PxP	PxP

Diagram 81
(White to play)

White sees at a glance that he can capture Black's Queen Pawn without having to fear Black's King Knight, which is pinned and therefore helpless. The proposition might be sound 999 times out of a thousand; here we have the thousandth case! Black's Queen Pawn is untouchable, as White finds out after:

6 NxP?	NxN!!

The staggering move that White never dreamt was possible! Black calmly surrenders the Queen.

7 BxQ	B—N5ch

And this of course is the point of the pitfall: White must interpose his Queen. His Queen Bishop has been decoyed from his native diagonal.

8 Q—Q2	KxB

Black can simply play 8 . . . BxQch with a piece ahead. But the more dramatic text move serves the same purpose, as White's Queen is pinned and must be lost.

"Must"? White tries a swindle.

9 R—B1	. . . .

If Black wants to play cat-and-mouse, he may make a careless move, allowing White to save his Queen by 10 R—B3! Many a player has been cheated of victory by such a lapse.

9	BxQch

Black is too wily!

10 KxB	. . . .

Black has an easy win with the extra piece.

In the next pitfall, from the Ruy Lopez, greed is punished in a way that is equally incisive but even more unorthodox. It requires imaginative powers out of the ordinary to devise such pitfalls.

1 P—K4	P—K4
2 N—KB3	N—QB3
3 B—N5	P—QR3
4 B—R4	P—Q3
5 BxNch	PxB

The Exchange has given Black an open Queen Knight file which he means to exploit; an irreproachable idea, if pursued within limits.

6	P—Q4	P—B3
7	N—B3	R—N1
8	Q—Q3	N—K2
9	B—K3!	. . . .

A strange-looking move. Has White been stricken with chess-blindness? How is it possible for him to deprive the Queen Knight Pawn of any protection in the face of Black's 7th move?

Diagram 82 (*Black to play*)

| 9 . . . . | | RxP |

Being greedy, Black asks no questions—or if he asks them, he does not look far for the answers. However, this is only the first part of the pitfall, and Black is by no means lost.

| 10 | PxP | BPxP |

The alternative 10 . . . QPxP?? loses a Rook. (How?)

| 11 | NxP! | . . . . |

But this is a real pitfall!

Since there is no obvious reason for the offer of the Knight, Black should apply himself to find the hidden reason for it.

His best course is 11 . . . B—K3, when he can still make a fight of it. But, as happens so often, greed has completely befuddled Black's wits.

(*See Diagram 83.*)

Diagram 83 (*Black to play*)

11	PxN?
12 QxQch	KxQ
13 Castles (Q)ch!	. . . .

This is the hidden point of the pitfall. White's castling wins the exposed Rook, leaving White the Exchange up.*

As for the question in the note to Black's 10th move: if *13 . . . QPxP??; 14* QxQch, KxQ; *15* Castles (Q)ch, and White wins a whole Rook.

In the following example from the Center Counter Game, Black greedily snatches a Pawn, equally blind to the consequences:

1 P—K4	P—Q4
2 PxP	QxP
3 N—QB3	Q—QR4
4 P—Q4	N—KB3
5 N—B3	B—N5
6 B—K2	N—B3
7 B—K3	Castles

Black has developed enterprisingly and rapidly. He now threatens to win a Pawn by *8 . . .* BxN; *9* BxB, NxP; *10* BxN, P—K4. The immediate *8 . . .* P—K4 may be even more formidable.

---

* The loser of this game, the exotically named Belgian master O'Kelly de Galway, later became one of Europe's best players.

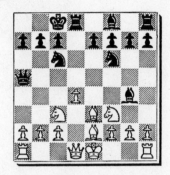

Diagram 84
(*White to play*)

The threat is not an easy one to parry. White defends in the Marshall manner—he sets a pitfall. As for Black, overconfident as he is of winning the Queen Pawn, he is not alert to the possibility of a pitfall.

> **8 N—Q2!**

A surprising reply.

> **8 . . . .   BxB**

Now one would expect 9 NxB, to guard the Queen Pawn. But in that case Black plays 9 . . . P—K4! with a strong initiative.

> **9 QxB!   . . . .**

This looks like a blunder leaving the Queen Pawn to its fate.

> **9 . . . .   NxP?**

Black is too greedy to resist temptation.

> **10 BxN   RxB**
> **11 N—N3   . . . .**

Only now does Black realize that he has been led on a fool's errand. White's Knight on QN3 forks Queen and Rook, leaving White with the Exchange for a Pawn—a winning material advantage (*Diagram 85*).

In the heat of the battle it is not always easy to restrain the

Diagram 85 (*Black to play*)

impulse to grab. But if you stop long enough to ask yourself, "What's he up to?" you will avoid many a pitfall.

PART THREE

GIMMICKS
in OVER-THE-BOARD PLAY

AN amusing story is told of the Hungarian master Balla who once announced a mate in two against his fellow Hungarian Breyer. The latter, a deep thinker, showed no reaction; if anything he seemed rather bored. Taken aback, Balla reexamined the position. Imagine his horror when he found there was no mate in two!

After some frenzied study of the position, Balla triumphantly announced a mate in three. Breyer was still bored. Once more Balla looked at the position, saw there was no mate in three, pondered and pondered and then . . . resigned!

So it is with chess gimmicks. They don't always work.

CHAPTER 8

Slick, Sly, and Subtle

Emanuel Lasker, who held the World's Championship title for twenty-seven years, wrote this telling passage some years after he lost the title: "Of my fifty-seven years I have applied at least thirty to forgetting most of what I have learned or read. Since then I have acquired a certain ease I should never again like to be without. If need be, I can increase my skill in chess; if need be I can do that of which I have no idea at present. I have stored little in my memory, but I can apply that little. I keep it in order, but resist every attempt to increase its dead weight."

All of us might envy Lasker his easy readiness to confront every difficult situation with such calm assurance. But there are times when even lesser players rise to the occasion, and display an insight worthy of a World's Champion. Take this example from the Carlsbad tournament of 1911:

1	P—Q4	P—Q4
2	N—KB3	B—B4
3	P—B4	P—QB3

In almost every variation of the Queen's Gambit Declined Black has trouble developing his Queen's Bishop. Here it seems that Black has solved this vexing problem quite satisfactorily. If White cannot exploit the position of the Black Queen's Bishop, then he has failed to gain anything from the initiative conferred by having the first move.

Carl Schlechter, one of the great masters of the period, is play-

ing White. How does he attempt to prove that the development
of Black's Bishop was faulty?

PERLIS

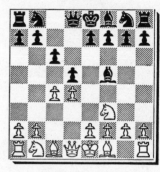

Diagram 86
(*White to play*)

SCHLECHTER

4 **Q—N3!**   . . . .

The logical move. White tries to exploit the absence of Black's
Queen Bishop from the Queen-side.

4 . . . .   **Q—N3**
5 **PxP**   . . . .

Forcing Black to exchange Queens, which gives White the
open Queen Rook file.

5 . . . .   **QxQ**
6 **PxQ**   . . . .

Only now does Black realize that his jaunty development of
the Queen Bishop may mean trouble for him. Thus if 6 . . .
PxP; 7 N—B3, N—KB3; 8 N—QN5, N—R3; 9 RxN!, PxR; 10 N—
B7*ch* and 11 NxR, winning some material no matter how Black
plays.

So Black tries a different way.

6 . . . .   **BxN**

Surely a common-sense move. The idea is that after 7 **RxB,**
PxP Black has avoided the inconvenient variation just given.

But White has a magnificent pitfall:

7 PxP!!   . . . .

PERLIS

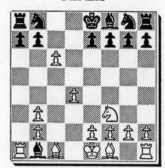

Diagram 87 (*Black to play*)

SCHLECHTER

Black's Queen Bishop is still under attack, and meanwhile
White threatens to win a Rook with 8 **PxP.**

The most economical defense is 7 . . . **B—K5.** Yet by playing
this logical-looking move Black would find himself in a subtle
pitfall: 8 **RxP!!, RxR;** 9 **P—B7** with the double threat of *10*
PxN(Q)ch and *10* **P—B8(Q)** mate. Thus after 7 . . . **B—K5??**
Black would be lost!

Luckily for Perlis, he saw the pitfall in good time and played:

7 . . . .   NxP!
8 RxB   . . . .

White's pitfall has netted him a clear Pawn to the good. There
is something paradoxical about Schlechter's pitfall. He saw it because he was a great master, and yet its chances of success were
spoiled because being a great master, he could not be suspected
of blundering away a piece! Perlis was on the alert, and this
helped him avoid the pitfall.

Here is another case—this time from the Mar del Plata tournament of 1953—where a great master is prevented from reaping the fruits of a really clever plan:

STEINER

Diagram 88
(*White to play*)

NAJDORF

Black has played one of his Knights to KB4 to prevent a White Knight from landing on Q6.* Nevertheless, White played 1 N—Q6! and Black replied . . . N—R3—to the unitiated, an utterly nonsensical sequence. Yet the moves make sense—

        1 N—Q6!   **. . . .**

Not a blunder but a pitfall! For if 1 . . . NxN; 2 PxN, QxP???; 3 N—N5! mates on the spot (or wins the Queen after 3 . . . P—N3) because of the double threat 4 QxRP mate and 4 NxBP mate!

After 1 . . . NxN; 2 PxN, Q—K1 Black would find himself in a disagreeable bind. This explains his choice of

        1 . . . .   **N—R3**

Still another mysterious Knight move, bumbling in appearance but sly in motivation, appears in the following position:

* Of such powerfully posted Knights the immortal Anderssen remarked, "They are like a rusty nail in your knee!"

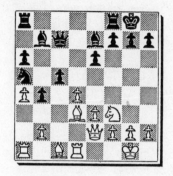

Diagram 89 (*Black to play*)

$$1 \ldots . \qquad \text{N—N6!!}$$

Absurd on the face of it, as White has a neat win of a Pawn now. But therein lies the pitfall!

$$2 \ \text{BxPch?} \qquad \text{KxB}$$
$$3 \ \text{Q—Q3ch} \qquad \ldots .$$

After 3 Q—B2*ch* we get the same continuation.

$$3 \ldots . \qquad \text{B—K5!!}$$

This is the surprise continuation that White completely overlooked!

Diagram 90
(*White to play*)

$$4 \ \text{QxBch} \qquad \ldots .$$

Worse—much worse—is 4 QxN???, P—B5!; 5 Q—R2, P—N6 and White has lost his Queen!

4 . . . .   P—B4!!

By menacing White's Queen Black gains time to win the Exchange.

5 Q—N1   NxR

Black's material advantage should win for him.

White's "mystery move" in the position of Diagram 91 shows that pitfalls are not always set by the attacker. White's position is more aggressive but at the moment he is embarrassed by the attack on his King Rook. To move this piece to R2—apparently White's only course—is to consign this Rook to long-term exile.

Diagram 91
(White to play)

White solves his problem with a slick maneuver:

1 Q—Q4!!   NxR??
2 R—KN6!   . . . .

Taking advantage of the fact that Black's Bishop Pawn is pinned, White swings over his Rook to force mate. Black has no defense!

An even more extraordinary example of a long-distance switch —this time with the Queen—appears in the following play:

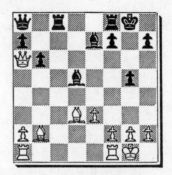

Diagram 92
(*White to play*)

Black has compromised his King-side by impetuously advancing his King Knight Pawn, allowing White's Bishops to rake the King-side. Banking on this irrevocable weakness, White sets a pitfall by seeming to ignore the double attack on his Pawn at KN2:

1 Q—R4! . . . .

Ignoring all the danger signs, Black plays:

1 . . . . BxNP

But White does not bother to move his attacked Rook.

2 Q—KN4!! Resigns

Black is beyond salvation, for example 2 . . . BxR; 3 BxPch!, KxB; 4 Q—R5ch, K—N1; 5 Q—R8 mate. Or 2 . . . B—B6; 3 Q—B5, KR—Q1; 4 QxRPch, K—B1; 5 Q—R8 mate!

Diagram 93 (*Black to play*)

Proceeding from one remarkable move to another, we come now to a Pawn march that is even more spectacular than the foregoing examples; see Diagram 93.

White's attack on the King-side is much more advanced than his opponent's counteraction on the other wing; so much so that White can set a neat pitfall that involves offering the Queen.

<table>
<tr><td>1 PxP!!</td><td>. . . .</td></tr>
</table>

Such unexpected moves have a psychological effect that is difficult to gauge. Some opponents are put on their guard, others lose their wits. Black, in this case, belongs in the second category.

<table>
<tr><td>1 . . . .</td><td>RxQ???</td></tr>
<tr><td>2 BxPch!</td><td>KxB</td></tr>
<tr><td>3 P—N8(Q)ch</td><td>K—R3</td></tr>
<tr><td>4 Q—N6 mate</td><td></td></tr>
</table>

A beautiful tribute to the inexhaustible variety of chess!

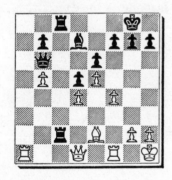

Diagram 94 (*Black to play*)

In Diagram 94 Black's control of the open Queen Bishop file gives him a won game, if he plays with reasonable care.

Unfortunately he chooses this ill-timed moment to dispose of White's precarious Queen Knight Pawn.

<table>
<tr><td>1 . . . .</td><td>BxP??</td></tr>
</table>

A trap. He thinks that White will reply 2 **QR—N1**, permitting a devastating retort in 2 . . . **BxB!**; 3 **QxB, QxR!**

But Black has overlooked a fine point:

2 QxR!   . . . .

This wins, for if 2 . . . **RxQ???;** *3* **R—R8***ch* leads to mate.

Again a Pawn lures a player to disaster in the following position:

Diagram 95 (*Black to play*)

Black sets a pitfall with:

1 . . . .   **P—K4!**

Though completely unguarded, this Pawn is best declined, for reasons that will become abundantly clear.

2 BxKP?   . . . .

White succumbs to temptation.

2 . . . .   **B—B4***ch*
3 **K—R1**   **R—K1!**

The light dawns. This move wins the reckless Bishop, which is tied to its present square. Thus if *4* **B—KB4??** Black wins the Queen with the discovered attack *4* . . . **N—N6***ch*.

Nor can White guard the unfortunate Bishop (*4* **Q—R5, P—KN3** and the Bishop is lost).

And again in Diagram 96, a Pawn advance proves Black's undoing, while another Pawn acts as decoy. As in Diagram 94, the loser tempts fate by blundering into a trap.

KOTOV

Diagram 96
(*White to play*)

STOLTZ

In this position from the World Championship interzonal tournament at Saltsjobaden in 1952, material is approximately even: White has Bishop and Knight against Rook and two Pawns.

Black's far-advanced Bishop Pawn has elements of strength and weakness. The weakness might be brought out by some such continuation as *1 N—Q2, R—KB1; 2 B—K6, P—Q5; 3 B—Q5.*

One thing is certain: White's Queen must remain at her present square, blockading the further advance of the potentially dangerous Pawn. But, as in so many other examples we have studied, White is too greedy:

1 QxRP??   . . . .

Sheer folly! He allows the Bishop Pawn to advance, threatening mate on the move and cutting the Queen off from the defense.

1 . . . .   P—B7!

Threatening 2 . . . R—N8 mate!

The reply 2 QxNPch is pointless, for then 2 . . . R—N2 wins the White Queen.

2 **B—N2**   . . . .

Or 2 N—N3, Q—B6ch; 3 B—N2 and now Black wins as in the next note.

2 . . . .   **Q—B6!!**

KOTOV

Diagram 97
(*White to play*)

STOLTZ

A lovely finish.

If 3 BxQ, R—N8 mate. Even prettier is 3 N—N3, P—B8(Q)ch!; 4 NxQ, QxB mate. Beautiful as this conclusion is, it highlights the fatally unsound character of 1 QxRP??

In Diagram 98 White commits the same blunder; but at least he has the excuse that his prey is more valuable than a Pawn, while the pitfall is subtler than the previous one. What is interesting about this pitfall is that its full consequences are not immediately apparent. Like some crimes, that start with stealing and end with murder, White's plan to win a Pawn ends with the win of a Bishop.

TIETZ

Diagram 98 (*Black to play*)

MAADER

White threatens **QxB** or **BxP***ch*. Most players would save the Bishop and let the Rook Pawn go. Black ignores the Rook Pawn, to be sure, but he ignores the Bishop as well!

| 1 . . . . | QR–B1!? |

Who is to foresee—certainly not White—that this Rook will administer checkmate in the not too remote future?!

| 2 QxB? | N–K4! |

This is the point of the pitfall: Black begins action against White's King, simultaneously attacking White's Queen.

| 3 Q–Q4 | . . . . |

Virtuously declining the distant Queen Rook Pawn; but White's Queen can accomplish precious little for the defense.

3	NxN*ch*
4 PxN	Q–N4*ch*
5 K–R1	B–R6
6 R–N1	. . . .

What does Black have to show now for his piece down?

He has the open lines and he has aggressive positions for his pieces menacing the exposed White King.

TIETZ

Diagram 99 (*Black to play*)

MAADER

6	QxRch!!
7 KxQ	R—B8ch
8 B—B1	RxB mate

In the last analysis, White's downfall was due to his undeveloped Queen-side. Such lack of development should cause you to think twice before plunging into complicated lines of play.

In Diagram 100, however, backward development leads to an-

WARD

Diagram 100
(*White to play*)

COLE

other kind of difficulty. White's Bishops point ominously at Black's King-side, but one of these Bishops—the fianchettoed one at QN2—cannot function usefully without substantial collaboration from Black.

If left to his own devices, Black will drive off White's Rook from K5 by playing . . . B—B3. This will also neutralize the long diagonal. Then Black will be able to continue his development with . . . N—Q3 and . . . B—B4.

We see, then, that if White is to make anything of his initiative, he must do it *right now*. So he sets a remarkably subtle pitfall:

1 Q—R5!   . . . .

Threatens mate—often an effective way to panic an opponent. There is a right way and a wrong way to answer the threat. The right way is 1 . . . N—B3! developing with gain of time, and without weakening the King's position. The wrong way—the way actually chosen by Black—opens up the King-side to the menacing though stealthy long-range action of the fianchettoed Bishop. The consequences are disastrous for Black.

1 . . . .   P—KN3??

White answers this with the kind of move that you fleetingly consider and then dismiss as mere daydreaming:

2 NxP!!!   . . . .

A difficult position! White's threat, now that the fianchettoed Bishop's diagonal is partly unmasked, is 3 QxRPch!!, KxQ; 4 R—R5ch, K—N1; 5 R—R8 mate!

The first dazzling possibility that occurs to us is 2 . . . PxQ; 3 BxPch?!, KxB???; 4 RxPch, K—N3; 5 N—B4 mate!

Though this line impressively demonstrates the power of the fianchettoed Bishop on the long diagonal, it is unsound. For after 2 . . . PxQ; 3 BxPch?!, Black escapes with 3 . . . K—R1! or 3 . . . K—N2!

The correct reply to 2 . . . PxQ is the prosaic 3 NxBch! Then if 3 . . . K—R1; 4 RxP dis ch, P—B3; 5 RxP mate. Or 3 . . . K—

WARD

Diagram 101
(*Black to play*)

COLE

N2; 4 RxP dis ch with the pretty alternatives 4 . . . P—B3; 5 RxP mate or 4 . . . N—B3; 5 RxP mate!

Best after 2 . . . PxQ (from Diagram 101); 3 NxBch is 3 . . . QxN. But then 4 RxQ leaves White with a Pawn ahead and an overwhelming positional advantage.

Flustered by all these possibilities, Black tries a desperate swindle which at least disposes of the immediate mating threat:

2 . . . .   QxN!?

WARD

Diagram 102
(*White to play*)

COLE .

3 Q—R6!!   . . . .

A delightfully delicate move. Black's Queen is still attacked and has no escape—for example 3 . . . Q—Q3; 4 QxRPch!! forcing mate.

In the event of 3 . . . B—B3 White contemptuously spares the Queen, playing 4 RxN!, Q—Q3; 5 BxB and Black is faced with three mating threats. One of them must succeed.

3 . . . .   B—Q1

As good or bad as anything else.

4 RxN!   Resigns

The triumph of the long diagonal, foolishly opened by Black when he played 1 . . . P—KN3?? Black can no longer stop mate.

Where this pitfall succeeded because it was so subtle, the pitfall that evolves from Diagram 103 is a success because it is so commonplace. This commonplace element reminds us of some of the most ingenious solutions in whodunits. The gimmick that explains everything is quite familiar, but it has been placed *in an unfamiliar context*.

HALLIWELL

Diagram 103
(*Black to play*)

CHAPMAN

In this position which turned up in a tournament at Ilford in England in 1953, Black played:

1 . . . .   **Q—K1!**

This move is standard procedure for Black in the Dutch Defense. Black's object, as White well knows, is to place the Queen aggressively at KR4.

Here, *1 . . . Q—K1* not only serves the purpose of development; it is the beginning of a slick pitfall. The move is made in broad daylight, and White is at liberty to search for the hidden purpose of the Queen maneuver. But like Poe's famous "purloined letter" which was left in the most obvious place, . . . **Q—K1** excites no attention because its object is so familiar.

2 N—Q2??   . . . .

Lulled into heedlessness by the thrice-familiar, White plays carelessly. By playing *2 P—K3* he would have warded off the worst.

2 . . . .   **N/2xBP!**

A complete surprise for Black's unwary opponent.

HALLIWELL

Diagram 104
(*Black to play*)

CHAPMAN

3 PxN   . . . .

Refusing the Knight leaves White a Pawn down without compensation—and that unattractive course was his best.

| 3 . . . . | BxP*ch* |
| 4 K—R1 | . . . . |

Now Black is almost ready for . . . Q—R4—but not quite.

| 4 . . . . | NxP*ch!* |
| **Resigns** | |

For after 5 PxN, Q—R4*ch* (at last!) forces mate! No wonder White failed to see anything sinister in the routine . . . Q—K1.

In Chapter 11 you will find more examples of players discovering they have been hoodwinked. Nothing in chess can be more entertaining—or more painful! It all depends on whose ox is gored.

CHAPTER 9

The Gentle Art of Swindling

Once upon a time a man brought a key to a hardware store and asked to have a duplicate made. The expert took the key, eyed it critically, and commented disparagingly, "This key shouldn't work."

"Maybe so," replied the customer, "but it does!"

That, in a single sentence, is pretty much the story of swindles. By all the rules, laws, principles, and ethics of chess, swindles ought to fail. Yet they work—not always, to be sure, but often enough, and quite effectively, too.

As we have pointed out, there is still a faint stigma attached to swindles. We all share the wistful belief that chess is a matter of abstract justice; and a man who has outplayed his opponent 99.99 per cent of the way is "morally" entitled to victory. However, as

Diagram 105
(*Black to play*)

long as chess games are decided by results, swindles will have their perfectly legitimate place in chess. Just as post-mortems cannot bring a corpse to life, so the most beautiful analysis in the world cannot annul those deadly words "checkmate" or "resign."

Our first swindle (Diagram 105) vividly brings out the value of swindles in staving off almost certain defeat.

If there was ever a position in which a player could resign with a clear conscience, here it is. Black is hopelessly behind in material, and stands to lose a Knight. Yet he has a fantastic resource, so powerful that White is able to achieve a laborious draw only after a whole series of problem moves!

$$1 \ldots \ldots \qquad \text{N—N5!!}$$

Disregarding the fact that his Queen is attacked, Black threatens 2 . . . QxP mate or 2 . . . RxR mate. The more you look at the position, the more convinced you become that *White* is lost! This is not true, but the fact is that he can save himself only by an extraordinary stroke. This is the lesson that we learn from swindles: while there's life there's hope, and many a seemingly lost position has unexpected assets.

$$2 \quad \text{Q—N8ch!!!} \qquad \ldots \ldots$$

Incomprehensible at first sight, this move is the only one to save the game for White!

Diagram 106
(*Black to play*)

White's last move, for all that it looks like a typographical error, is based on a sound idea. After 2 . . . KxQ??; 3 RxRch, KxR; 4 RxQ or 2 . . . RxQ??; 3 RxQ both Black mating threats have disappeared and he is faced with the stark fact that he is the Exchange down.

So Black nonchalantly plays:

$$2 . . . . \qquad \text{K—N3!}$$

This sets a really delectable pitfall. Suppose White tries 3 R—QB6ch??! hoping for 3 . . . QxR?? when 4 QxR wins easily. Black answers 3 R—QB6ch??! with 3 . . . K—R4!!

After 3 . . . K—R4!! White discovers that he is still subject to two mating threats and his Queen and both Rooks are attacked. The desperate 4 R—B5ch leaves Black with a forced win after 4 . . . P—N4!

This explains why White is very happy to have a forced draw in the position of Diagram 107:

Diagram 107
(*White to play*)

$$3 \ \text{Q—K6ch!} \qquad \text{K—R2}$$
$$4 \ \text{Q—N8ch!!!} \qquad \text{Drawn!}$$

Not every swindle is as spectacular as this one and some often fail. But they are certainly worth trying. Diagram 108 shows one that was tried some years ago against the German master, Kurt Richter, in a game in which he gave Rook odds. A wizard of chess tactics, Richter made a wonderful fight at the odds, and, as you can see, his King Pawn is due for promotion.

AMATEUR

Diagram 108
(*White to play*)

RICHTER

Still a Rook down, Richter tries his only chance—making use of the far-advanced King Pawn.

1 N—B5ch   . . . .

To his horror, Black sees that after *1 . . . K—B1???; 2 P—K7ch, K—K1; 3 N—Q6ch* the terrible Pawn queens.

True, *1 . . . K—K1!* forces a draw: *2 N—Q6ch, K—K2; 3 N—B5ch, K—K1; 4 N—Q6ch.* Had Black adopted this line, Richter's swindle would have been amply justified.

But Black sees an ingenious winning method—and this brings out the real point of Richter's swindle.

1 . . . .   **K—B3!**

Contemplating an ingenious way to lose.

2 P—K7!?   **BxN???**

By playing *2 . . . B—Q2!* Black still wins.
(*See Diagram 109.*)

Black is all set to answer *3 P—K8(Q)???* with *3 . . . R—R7 mate!* Very neat, but White has an even neater move:

3 P—K8(N) mate!

White's swindle is picturesque but rather off the beaten track.

AMATEUR

Diagram 109
(*White to play*)

RICHTER

Here is one that is both routine and exemplifies a motif that often turns victory into defeat.

WINAWER

Diagram 110
(*White to play*)

BLACKBURNE

Winawer, completely outplayed and faced with the queening of White's passed Pawn, had set up a delightful swindle. The line of play that Winawer had prepared bears out his reputation as a wit. Here is the variation:

1 **P—N8(Q)??**   . . . .

A blunder—believe it or not!

1	**Q—B8ch!!**

If now 2 **QxQ**, Black is stalemated!

2 **K—R2**	**Q—KB5ch!!**

And now a second stalemate feature! If White plays 3 **QxQ**, Black is stalemated!

Nor does this exhaust Black's drawing resources: if 3 **P—N3**, **QxBPch** and Black draws by perpetual check!

3 **K—N1**	**Q—B8ch!!**

And the position is a draw!

But—and this is the important point—Blackburne was not taken in by the swindle. He studied the position in Diagram 121 appreciatively and then, falling in with the spirit of the occasion, reached out as if to queen the Pawn. Then he suddenly swung around his hand and played 1 **BxNch!** killing the stalemate possibility. The game ended with the hearty laughter of spectators and players alike.

AMATEUR

Diagram 111
(*White to play*)

SCHLOESSER

Some swindles are remarkably subtle—anything but easy to see through. Consider the following, for example—from a game between two amateurs!

White has two Pawns for the Exchange, so that we may consider material academically even. But the doubled and isolated Queen Rook Pawns cannot last very long, so there is little doubt that White has a lost game.

Certainly Schloesser had no illusions about the position, and therefore set about devising one of the most far-reaching swindles in the history of chess. As is usually the case in really outstanding swindles, the first move is thoroughly enigmatic:

1 K—B1!!   . . . .

Had Black been a mind reader, he would have played 1 . . . N—Q4! with an easy win.

1 . . . .   **RxP??**
2 B—N4!!   . . . .

This attacks the Rook, of course, but it also embodies a threat Black does not even dream of.

Before you see how the swindle unfolds, you must bear in mind that White enjoys an advantage here that Schlechter

AMATEUR

Diagram 112
(*White to play*)

SCHLOESSER

lacked in the position of Diagram 87. There we pointed out that an incomprehensible move by a master is treated with respect, whereas an incomprehensible move by an amateur is dismissed as . . . an incomprehensible move. Consequently Black does not pause to examine the position, but grabs thoughtlessly:

2 . . . .   **RxRP**

Threatening to win White's Queen with . . . R—R8. In contrast to White's seemingly irrational play, Black's moves seem models of common-sense procedure.

3 **Q—R6ch!!!**   . . . .

The end of an illusion—though on the face of it this move makes no more sense than White's previous ones.

3 . . . .   **KxQ**

After 3 . . . K—B2; 4 QxRPch, K—K3 White has a two-move mate.

4 B—B8ch	K—R4
5 P—N4ch	K—R5
6 B—K7ch	P—N4
7 BxPch	K—R6

AMATEUR

Diagram 113
(*White to play*)

SCHLOESSER

The Black King walks the plank. Only now can we appreciate the exquisite subtlety of White's 1 K—B1!! which prevents Black from playing . . . K—N7.

8	N—B2*ch*	KxRP
9	B—B4 mate!	

Another classic swindle, not quite as deep as this one, but more rewarding because of the blunders on both sides, occurred in an offhand game played at St. Petersburg in 1900.

The setting for this swindle is Diagram 114. White is a Pawn down and his Pawn position is so weakened that with normal, uneventful play he is sure to lose. White (Tchigorin) sets a wonderfully ingenious swindle, which, however, has a great gaping hole. Yet Black, given the opportunity of escaping scot-free and with a bonus of a whole Rook or Knight, falls ingloriously!

SCHUMOFF

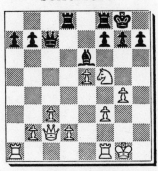

Diagram 114
(*White to play*)

TCHIGORIN

1	RxP??!	. . . .

The swindle.

1	. . . .	Q—N3*ch*
2	K—N2	. . . .

Black is in clover. By playing 2 . . . BxN! he has a clear win, as White's Rook at QR7 is still under attack.

Instead, he plays an astonishingly careless move against a great master of the attack.

2 . . . .   **QxR???**

Now the swindle works.

3 **N—K7ch**   **K—R1**

SCHUMOFF

Diagram 115
(White to play)

TCHIGORIN

4 **QxPch!!**   **KxQ**
5 **R—KR1 mate!**

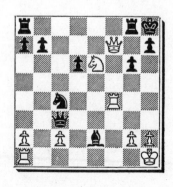

Diagram 116
(White to play)

And in the next example too, Black is more to be pitied than scorned. A piece ahead (see Diagram 116), he has to play with a certain amount of care because White's pieces exert an uncomfortable pressure.

White's Rook at QR1 is under attack and he has to move it somewhere. The Rook move gives us the same motif as in Diagram 103. There Black's Queen move, which started a subtle pitfall, passed for a developing move. Here White's Rook move, which passes for a would-be defensive move, turns out to be the prelude to a sly swindle.

1 R(R1)—RKB1!?   . . . .

This Rook should NOT be captured. But Black sees the Rook move as a sheer blunder.

1	BxR???
2 QxRPch!!!	KxQ
3 R—R4 mate	

Now Black gets the point of the swindle. If his Bishop were still at K7, he could interpose at KR4!

The endgame is the special domain of the swindle, for it is in this final stage that players dream up last-minute expedients to save themselves from otherwise certain loss. Some of the cleverest gimmicks we know have been concocted in positions that most players would have considered resigning. What, for example, makes it worth while for White to continue playing in the position of Diagram 117?

White's situation (from a game played in the Monte Carlo tournament of 1904) seems hopeless. The well-supported, passed Queen Knight Pawn needs only two moves to queen. White's Rook is badly placed, and his short-hopping Knight shows to poor advantage against the long-range Bishop. Nevertheless, a plucky fighter like Marshall can work wonders with even such scrawny material.

MARCO

Diagram 117
(*White to play*)

MARSHALL

But how? If *1 RxPch, K—N1; 2 P—B6, PxP; 3 RxP, P—N7* and White cannot hold out much longer.

Marshall's method is much subtler, and has the advantage of creating difficulties for his opponent.

1 P—B6!?   . . . .

This should still lose—but only after Black has exerted himself to the utmost by *1 . . . PxP; 2 RxPch, K—N1; 3 R—N7ch!, KxR; 4 N—B5ch, K—R2!!; 5 NxR, B—Q5; 6 K—B3, K—R3; 7 K—K4, K—R4!; 8 KxB, KxN* and the Queen Knight Pawn must queen.

MARCO

Diagram 118
(*Black to play*)

MARSHALL

Does this stamp the swindle as a failure? Not at all. A good swindle should have a maximum and a minimum objective. The maximum objective is of course to transform a loss into a win. But the minimum objective is to make the opponent's task more arduous and complicated, to bewilder him with obscure alternatives, to raise doubts in his mind about the accuracy of his judgment.

1 . . . .   B—K4??

The swindle has worked! Missing the rather difficult win just pointed out, Black adopts an ultra-careful line which rules out all possibility of his winning the game, and even makes his ultimate defeat likely.

2 PxPch   K—N1

He has no choice, for if 2 . . . KxP??; 3 N—B5ch wins the Rook. We are beginning to realize that White's Knight is exceptionally agile.

3 N—B5   R—R7ch
4 K—R3   P—N7

MARCO

Diagram 119
(White to play)

MARSHALL

And now it might well seem that White has exhausted his resources and that Marco was right after all. But Marshall has only begun to fight. He is prepared to let the Black Pawn queen—for a price!

5 R—K7! . . . .

Now White's Rook becomes active. He permits 5 . . . P—N8(Q)?? in order to continue 6 R—K8ch, K—R2; 7 R—QR8ch, K—N3; 8 P—N8(Q)ch winning Black's Queen and the game.

5 . . . . **K—R2**

Threatening to queen safely.

6 R—K8 . . . .

Marshall parries by being ready to transpose into the note to his 5th move in the event of Black's queening his Pawn.

6 . . . . **P—B3**

Guarding the queening square of White's Queen Knight Pawn. This calls forth a dazzling display of Marshall's combinative powers.

7 R—QR8ch! **K—N3**
8 RxR! **P—N8(Q)**

MARCO

Diagram 120
(*White to play*)

MARSHALL

In this apparently hopeless position Marshall gives us the last finesse of his swindle:

9	P—N8(Q)ch!	BxQ
10	R—QN2ch!	QxR
11	N—R4ch	K—N4
12	NxQ	. . . .

By turning back to Diagram 117 you can appreciate the wizardry of Marshall's achievement. There the ending was "definitely" lost for him. Now, after 12 NxQ, he is out of all his troubles, with a Pawn to the good in an endgame which gives Black laborious drawing possibilities. This is swindling in the grand manner!

An echo of Marshall's swindle is the amusing feature of the ending that starts from Diagram 121. Realizing that he is powerless against the far-advanced passed Pawn, Black decides that a swindle is his only chance:

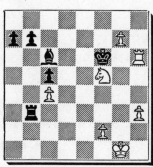

Diagram 121
(*Black to play*)

1	KxN!?

The swindle. White can now win easily with 2 RxB! forcing the safe queening of his Knight Pawn. Instead, all too sure of victory, he plays carelessly.

2 P—N8(Q)??	. . . .

Now Black's swindle works:

2	R—N8ch

3	K—R2	R—R8*ch*
4	K—N3	R—KN8*ch*
5	K—R4	RxQ
	Resigns	

Another example in which a passed Pawn plays a role is seen in Diagram 122; but in this case the passed Pawn saves the day for the swindler.

Diagram 122
(*Black to play*)

With a Knight and Pawn ahead, White has an easy win. Instead of resigning, Black tries a swindle.

$$1 \ . \ . \ . \ . \qquad \textbf{PxP!?}$$

Now White should simply play 2 **PxP**, squelching the swindle at once. But the bait looks too attractive:

$$2 \ \textbf{N—Q7???} \qquad . \ . \ . \ .$$

This tempting Knight fork loses by force!

$$2 \ . \ . \ . \ . \qquad \textbf{PxP}ch$$

Now the light dawns. If 3 **RxP**, **R—N8***ch* and mate next move. So White tucks his King away in the corner.

$$3 \ \textbf{K—R1} \qquad \textbf{R—N8!}$$

Smashing an illusion; for if 4 **RxR**, **P—B8(Q)***ch;* 5 **RxQ, RxR**

mate. (If Black wants to rub it in, he can promote to a Rook and still force mate!)

Diagram 123
(*White to play*)

4 R–R1	. . . .

Even this abject resource fails.

4	RxR/R8
5 RxR	P–B8(Q)*ch*
6 RxQ	RxR mate!

A delightful example of what Nimzovich used to call "the passed Pawn's lust to expand." It is a devastating comment on White's greediness that he never had time to capture either of the forked Rooks.

Diagram 124
(*Black to play*)

Our final swindle also depends on the use—or rather the misuse—of a passed Pawn. The position of Diagram 124 is quite lost for Black. White must obtain a destructive passed Pawn, and Black's Queen is far from the scene of action.

If 1 . . . Q—B7; 2 PxP!, QxRch; 3 K—R2 and Black can resign. Or 1 . . . R—KN1; 2 P—N7ch, K—R2; 3 Q—Q3 mate. Clearly a swindle is called for:

$$1 \ . \ . \ . \ . \qquad\qquad \textbf{PxP!?}$$

A frail reed for Black to lean on, as 2 P—B7! decides at once: 2 . . . R—KB1; 3 QxP and it's all over.

$$2 \ \textbf{QxP???} \qquad\qquad . \ . \ . \ .$$

Now the swindle works. White intends to make ingenious use of a pin, overlooking a more effective counterpin at Black's disposal.

$$2 \ . \ . \ . \ . \qquad\qquad \textbf{R—KN1}$$

This seems to win the Queen, but White has no fear. He has in mind what seems to him a thoroughly crushing move:

$$3 \ \textbf{R—Q8} \qquad\qquad . \ . \ . \ .$$

Very plausible—Black's Rook is pinned, White threatens three mates on the move, and 3 . . . RxR?? is of course answered by 4 Q—N7 mate.

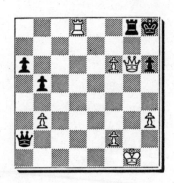

Diagram 125
(*Black to play*)

3 . . . .   **Q—N8ch!**

The brutal counterpin brings Black back to reality. He resigns, for Black will continue 4 **QxQ** leaving White nothing to play for.

From the examples in this chapter we see that swindles, properly used, sometimes hold out hope of saving what is otherwise a hopelessly lost game. A word or two of caution is in order. The proper time for a swindle is when your position seems hopeless. You gain little, and stand to lose a great deal, by resorting to trappy play in positions that promise victory by less sensational means. In the final section of this book you will see some graphic examples of what happens when a gimmick is topped by a better gimmick.

And the best way to avoid swindles set by your opponent? Tarrasch's advice is still best: "Sit on your hands!" Almost every successful swindle owes its success to hasty, careless play on the part of the prospective winner. You owe it to yourself not to relax your vigilance on the brink of victory. The simple question, "What's he up to?" will avoid many a heartbreaking loss.

PART FOUR

GIMMICK vs. GIMMICK

WHEN Alexander the Great set out to conquer Persia, he sent the following message to the king of Persia: "I, Alexander, consider the whole of thy treasure, and the whole of thy land to be mine."

Some twenty-three centuries later another great Alexander—Alexander Alekhine—had this to say about his first tournament game: "It endowed me with a curious psychological weakness which I have had to work long and hard to eradicate—if indeed I ever have eradicated it!—the impression that I could always, or nearly always, when in a bad position, conjure up some unexpected combination to extricate me from my difficulties. A dangerous delusion."

Indeed it is. Confidence is an important asset to a chessplayer, but it can become a handicap when it prevents him from making allowances for the resourcefulness of his opponent.

CHAPTER 10

"He Sees It!"

The World Championship matches of 1935 and 1937 between
Alekhine and Euwe emphasized the importance of gimmicks
more strongly than any similar contests in the history of chess.
Time and again Alekhine owed his victory to surprise moves that
were good enough to baffle Euwe, himself a first-class tactician.
Alekhine's pitfalls caught Euwe off base repeatedly; his swindles
saved him more than once in desperate situations. Euwe lost
games by misjudging positions that were by no means unfavorable to him.

Euwe readily admitted his faults. "In one quality I was defi-
cient," he commented frankly; "the ability to distinguish between
the inspired and the unsound, between the daringly complicated
and the merely risky."

So we see that even World Champions can lose games by their
lack of insight in a single crucial move. In the case of lesser players, it is even more important to develop the knack of seeing
through pitfalls and parrying them advantageously. The object
of the concluding part of this book is to give you some valuable
practice in appraising tricky positions and avoiding your opponent's pitfalls—possibly turning them to your own advantage at
times.

Even Marshall, ingenious as he was, often had to admit failure
after setting one of his ingenious pitfalls. This happened repeatedly in his match with Capablanca in 1909. You can see an impressive example of this in Diagram 126.

Marshall, a Pawn down, tries to complicate matters for his comparatively inexperienced opponent.

CAPABLANCA

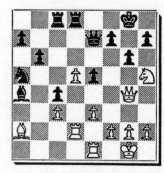

Diagram 126
(*White to play*)

MARSHALL

1 P—Q6!?	. . . .

So that if *1 . . . RxP??; 2 QxRch* wins.

1	Q—K3
2 Q—N5!?	. . . .

Now the capture of the shaky Queen Pawn seems feasible, but after *2 . . . RxP??; 3 RxR, QxR; 4 Q—R6!* White threatens *5 Q—N7 mate* and wins right off. (*4 . . . PxN* loses the Queen.)

Note that although this pitfall will fail, Marshall did not set it out of mere caprice. Had he played *2 QxQ, PxQ* the resulting endgame would have been lost for him in view of his disadvantage in material.

2	K—R1!

Forcing White's Knight to move and thus putting an end to the mate threat.

3 N—B6	RxP

Now the Pawn can be captured safely. Black is two Pawns to the good, and has successfully survived the complications.

Capablanca himself set many a pitfall during his long career. One of the subtlest of these appears in the position of Diagram 127, from a game at Bad Kissingen in 1928:

NIMZOVICH

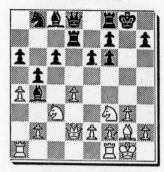

Diagram 127
(*White to play*)

CAPABLANCA

Black's King is somewhat insecure because his King-side Pawns are broken up. Capablanca takes advantage of this by:

    1 Q—R6!   . . . .

This sets an insidious pitfall. It appeals not to Black's greed, but to his caution. It seems the most natural thing in the world for him to safeguard his King by playing . . . K—R1 followed by . . . R—N1 and . . . R—N3, driving away the obnoxious Queen. But in that case, White has a brilliant winning line:

    1 . . . .   K—R1???
    2 N—K4!   B—K2

If 2 . . . P—KB4; 3 N—B6 forces Black to give up his Queen to stop mate.

    3 N/B3—N5!!   . . . .

A beautiful move, played to make room for his Bishop.

    3 . . . .   PxN

Forced to stop mate.

4 N—B6!!   . . . .

Another beautiful sacrifice with the same purpose as the previous sacrifice.

4 . . . .   **BxN**
5 B—K4!!   . . . .

Forcing checkmate.

What actually happened in Diagram 127? Nimzovich took one look at the position after *1* **Q—R6** and quietly played *1* **. . . BxN**, avoiding the fatal line just pointed out.

A simple pitfall, but one well worth knowing, appears in Diagram 128. With two minor pieces against Rook and Pawn, Black has a slight advantage in material. This is outweighed, however, by the strong position of White's Rooks on the open Queen Bishop file and the insecure position of Black's King.

Diagram 128
(*White to play*)

White plays his Rook to the seventh rank, apparently giving up his strong passed Pawn:

1 R—B7   . . . .

Black can now play *1* **. . . QxP??**. Instead, he moved his

Queen to N4. Had he grabbed the Pawn, he would have fallen into this pitfall:

1	QxP??
2 R—B8ch!	NxR
3 RxNch	K—K2

Black's Rook is tied to its present square in order to guard his Queen; that is what makes the pitfall possible.

4 RxR	. . . .

The result of the pitfall is that White is the Exchange to the good, and should win in due course. This type of exploitation of overburdened pieces is often seen in practical play.

The occasions on which Morphy fell into a pitfall were few and far between; for that matter, the pitfalls sprung by his opponents usually had a bad flaw. Characteristic is this one, shown on Diagram 129:

DE RIVIERE

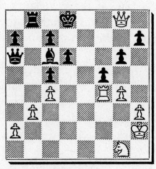

Diagram 129
(*Black to play*)

MORPHY

Both Kings are in some danger. Black can defend with *1* **B—K1**, but White's position is definitely more promising after *2* **R—B2**. So Black sets a pitfall:

$$1 \ldots \ldots \qquad \textbf{K—Q2!?}$$

This is the kind of position where an inexperienced player is likely to snap at the Rook thus presented to him.

In any event, Morphy refused the generous gift, and continued 2 QxRPch!, K—B1; 3 R—B2, winning in due course. Why did he spurn the Rook? Had he captured the Rook, play would have proceeded:

2 QxR??	QxRPch
3 K—N3	P—N4!

Threatening . . . Q—KN7 mate.

4 R—B2	. . . .

Does this stop the mate?

4	P—B5ch!
5 RxP	Q—N7 mate!

A very neat pitfall, worthy of a better success than it actually had. But, as we have shown, Morphy declined the Rook.*

This pitfall is a very useful one to study in some detail. In Diagram 129 you see at a glance that it is White who has the initiative, while Black's King is miserably harried. Yet, once the pitfall starts, White is mated on the 5th move. Why this sudden transformation?

A shrug of the shoulders, or some such comment as "the fortunes of war" will not explain the violent change. The real reason is White's 2 QxR??, which puts White's Queen hopelessly *out of play*. Suddenly Black's King is no longer persecuted, and the Black Queen and Bishop, previously mere onlookers, spring into action.

Before White can take the Rook, he must ask himself the standard question, "What's he up to?" as well as at least one more question: "Once my Queen is out of play, can my other

---

* This game, by the way, was played in 1863, after Morphy had withdrawn from serious play. Despite his lack of practice, he still retained his keen eye for tactical details.

pieces bear the weight of their defensive burden?" The player who does not ask such questions consistently will find himself constantly victimized by trappy play.

This advice is just as useful to masters as it is to average players. Take this instance of a World Champion going wrong—spectacularly wrong. When Steinitz was annotating a game from the New York tournament of 1889, he pointed out how one of the players could—and should—have captured a Pawn. Yet this capture would have led to a fast forced mate! Here is the position:

TCHIGORIN

Diagram 130
(*Black to Play*)

WEISS

With his first move, Black sets a deep pitfall:

1	. . . .	**P—N5!!**
2	**BPxP**	**PxP**

Weiss, seeing through the pitfall, now played 3 **RxR!**, and the game ended in a draw.

Here is what would have happened if Weiss had followed the Steinitz recipe:

3 **PxP???**   . . . .

What is hopelessly wrong about this move is that it opens the Queen Rook file all the way, at a time when White's Rooks are cut off from contact with the Queen-side. White's King is therefore at the mercy of enemy pieces.

3 . . . .   **R—R8ch!!**

This is the move that Steinitz missed. When you are unaware of a pitfall, such strokes are astounding. When you have broken down a pitfall into its component parts, these moves come as a matter of course.

TCHIGORIN

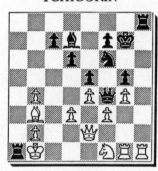

WEISS
(*variation*)

Diagram 131
(*White to play*)

4 **KxR**   . . . .

The march to the scaffold. If 4 K—B2, Q—B8 mate (or . . . R—B8 mate. Here you see the effect of the White King's separation from his Rooks).

4 . . . .   **Q—B8ch**

Again taking advantage of the helplessness of the White Rooks.

5 **K—R2**   **R—R1ch**

Triumph of the open file—the consequence of 3 PxP???

6 **B—R4**   **B—K3ch**

7 **P—N3**   **RxB mate**

White's pinned Queen Knight Pawn has no defensive value at all.

In a famous game played a few years later, in the Hastings tournament of 1895, the dangers of playing the Queen far from the scene of action were brought out in an even more compelling fashion than in Diagram 129:

TARRASCH

Diagram 132
(*White to play*)

PILLSBURY

Here there is no simple problem of a superficial player who carelessly disregards his defenses and sends his Queen gallivanting to the other wing. Black has set up a solid defensive position, and it is not clear how White can organize an attack quickly.

Furthermore, Black's threatened massacre of the Queen-side Pawns poses critical problems for White. If he tries *1 R—R1*, then *1 . . . Q—B7* follows with crushing effect. When this game was being played, all those present—with the exception of Pillsbury, of course—were sure that White was lost.

1 N—N4! . . . .

White must rely on pitfalls. If now *1 . . . QxP?; 2 NxP!, PxN; 3 QxBPch* with a winning attack (*3 . . . R—N2; 4 R—N4* winning or *3 . . . K—N1; 4 R—N4ch* winning).

1 . . . .   **N—Q2**

Wisely rejecting the bait and giving the King Bishop Pawn needed protection. White must find a new pitfall.

2 R/B4—B2!!   . . . .

Here it is—and very deep, too. How many players would be aware that 2 . . . QxP? is out of the question?

TARRASCH

Diagram 133
(*Black to play*)

PILLSBURY

After a careful study of the position, Tarrasch played 2 . . . K—N1. He eventually lost the game, but only because of a serious error of judgment later on. What would have happened if he had accepted White's challenge? Here is the play that would have ensued:

2 . . . .   **QxP?**
3 **N—B4!**   . . . .

White must act incisively before Black's Queen has a chance to get back into the game. The Knight move attacks Black's Bishop and also threatens to win the Exchange with N—N6*ch*.

3 . . . .   **B—B2**
4 **N—N6***ch*   **BxN**
5 **PxB**   . . . .

Threatens mate. With his Queen out of play, Black is unable to defend himself.

TARRASCH

Diagram 134
(*Black to play*)

PILLSBURY
(*variation*)

Black has two possible lines of defense, both of them inadequate. Thus if 5 . . . P—R3; 6 NxRP! (threatening 7 N—B7 dbl ch, K—N1; 8 Q—R8 mate!), PxN; 7 QxRPch, K—N1; 8 R—B5! And Black is helpless against the coming 9 R—R5. It is the absence of Black's Queen that reduces him to this helpless state.

Another way is 5 . . . N—B1; 6 NxP!, PxN; 7 RxP, K—N1; 8 R—B7 and wins. Again Black is powerless, this time against the coming 9 Q—R6. (If 8 . . . NxP; 9 QxP mate.)

But, as we have pointed out, Tarrasch saw through these variations and avoided them in the position of Diagram 133 by playing 2 . . . K—N1. In this way he not only escaped the sacrificial variations; he also left open the possibility of *getting the Queen back into play* by . . . Q—B3.

Good pitfalls are those which improve your position, or at least do it no harm, in the event that the prospective victim refuses to be "taken for a ride." This point is effectively illustrated in the following position from a game played in the British Championship of 1948:

THOMAS

Diagram 135
(*Black to play*)

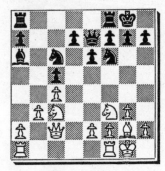

GOLOMBEK

Black has a perfectly natural desire to play . . . P—Q4, as he does not care to be left with a backward Pawn on the open Queen file. However, this exemplary positional move has a tactical drawback—it can result in the loss of a Pawn. After careful calculation Thomas convinces himself that the Pawn snatch would be disastrous for White, and he therefore continues:

1	P—Q4!
2 PxP	PxP

This is the pitfall position. Golombek saw the pitfall and played 2 KR—K1, to which Thomas replied 2 . . . QR—B1 and the game continued 3 QR—Q1, P—Q5; 4 N—QR4, N—QN5 with a promising game for Black.

In other words, White's avoidance of the pitfall left Black with excellent prospects.

Now for the pitfall itself, arising from Diagram 135 after the moves 1 . . . P—Q4!; 2 PxP, PxP:

3 N—KN5	. . . .

Apparently very strong, the threat being 4 NxQP, NxN???; 5 QxRP mate.

3	P—N3!

Stops the mate, and holds out the Queen Pawn as bait.

THOMAS

Diagram 136
(*White to play*)

GOLOMBEK
(*variation*)

| | 4 NxQP?? | . . . . |

A costly capture.

| | 4 . . . . | NxN |
| | 5 BxN | . . . . |

Naturally White does not fear 5 . . . QxN because of 6 BxN. But Black has a much stronger move.

| | 5 . . . . | N—N5! |

Now White has three pieces under attack. He saves everything —momentarily!—with:

| | 6 Q—K4! | . . . . |

So that if 6 . . . QxN?; 7 BxR. But White's last move has still a further point—it attacks Black's Queen.

| | 6 . . . . | NxB! |

The move on which the pitfall is based: Black's Queen is protected!

	7 QxN	KR—Q1

Now the pitfall enters its second phase: White is to lose material by force!

	8 Q—B6	. . . .

Counterattack on the Bishop.

	8	B—N2
	9 Q—N5	. . . .

Grimly clinging to the Bishop. Black must find a way to shake the Queen loose from her stubborn pursuit of the Bishop.

THOMAS

Diagram 137
(*Black to play*)

GOLOMBEK
(*variation*)

	9	QR—N1!
	10 P—KR4	P—R3
	11 N—R3	. . . .

Or *11* N—B3, BxN and wins.

	11	B—N7!
	12 QxR	. . . .

Else he loses the Knight. Thus ends the unequal struggle of White's Queen against Black's Queen, Bishop, and both Rooks.

12	RxQ
13 KxB	QxKP

With a Queen for Rook and Knight Black has a technically easy win. Thomas deserves credit for setting up this pitfall, and Golombek deserves equal credit for avoiding it.

The delightfully complicated play that revolved about Black's offer of a Pawn in this last example reminds us of the saying that Pawn sacrifices are more refined than Queen sacrifices. As we have seen, many a pitfall starts with the offer of a Pawn with malice aforethought. Often these pitfalls look harmless or incomprehensible. Take this one from the Belgrade tournament of 1952:

O'KELLY

Diagram 138
(*White to play*)

PIRC

White's King Pawn is attacked. Instead of defending the Pawn, White nonchalantly plays:

1 B—KB4!   . . . .

Pitfall or blunder? At all events, O'Kelly did not dream of capturing the tempting Pawn, and played *1* . . . N—K1 instead.

This is what would have happened if he had succumbed to temptation:

1	NxP??
2 R—K1!	. . . .

Wins a piece. The proof: 2 . . . P—B4; 3 NxB dbl *ch* etc. Or 2 . . . N—Q3; 3 NxBch and 4 BxN. Finally, if 2 . . . N—B3; 3 NxBch, NxN; 4 QxQ and 5 RxN.

Sometimes warnings are posted to keep us from snatching at dangerous Pawns. Capturing the Queen Knight Pawn is a familiar failing that has been the prelude to many a pitfall. And so prudence is White's best bet in Diagram 139:

Diagram 139
(*White to play*)

Black has just played 1 . . . B—Q2 tempting White to capture the Queen Knight Pawn. White wisely continued his development with 2 N—B3.

Had he played 2 QxP??, the sequel would have been 2 . . . B—QB3; 3 Q—N3, BxNP followed by . . . BxR. Not a very deep pitfall, but time and again careless players are taken in by the sinister Queen Knight Pawn. Disagreeable experience seems to leave no lasting impression—as in the case of the little boy who said, "Memory is the thing I forget with!"

Another type of pitfall with Pawns involves a surprise advance which is apparently impossible or at any rate inadvisable. Such pitfalls are often highly profitable because of their surprise value. Here is one from the United States Junior Championship of 1948:

POSCHEL

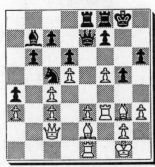

Diagram 140
(*White to play*)

CROSS

White resorts to an advance which most players would have labeled "impossible."

1 P—K4! . . . .

On any orthodox view of the matter, this advance is out of the question, as the Pawn is protected only once, and attacked three times. Yet Black, after due consideration, tamely replied 1 . . . P—KB3. Why?

There are two ways to capture the King Pawn. If 1 . . . QxP?; 2 B—Q3! and Black's Queen is trapped, and 2 . . . QxRch; 3 BxQ, RxBch; 4 K—B2 is greatly in White's favor.

Even worse for Black is 1 . . . NxP??; 2 B—Q3! pinning and winning the foolhardy Knight.

In the next example White advances in somewhat similar fashion to bring about an even more unusual kind of decision.

It would seem absolutely pointless for White to play 1 P—K5, which "simply" loses a Pawn. But that is what White does:

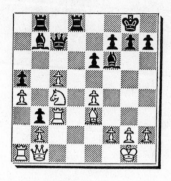

Diagram 141
(*White to play*)

1 P—K5!   **B—K2**

Why this tame reply? Because after *1 . . . BxKP??; 2 NxB, QxN; 3 P—B6!, B—R1; 4 P—B7* White forks both Rooks!

Equally "nonsensical" at first sight is White's advance in the following position:

Diagram 142
(*White to play*)

White "gives away" a Pawn by playing:

1 P—Q5!   **BxN**

But not *1 . . . NxP??; 2 NxBch!* and White wins a piece after *2 . . . NxN; 3 BxB* or *2 . . . QxN; 3 BxB, QxB; 4 QxN.*

2 BxB	N—K2

And Black has avoided a nasty pitfall.

Here is still another Pawn offer which like the previous one is based on an "optical illusion":

Diagram 143
(*White to play*)

In this position White can play *1 B—R3!* allowing *1 . . . BxP??*

Black's reliance on this "clever" reply might be based on the optical illusion that after *2 BxN, QxB; 3 RxB* he does not lose a piece because of *3 . . . QxN*. But this of course is wrong. To recapitulate:

1 B—R3!	BxP??
2 BxN	QxB
3 RxB	QxN
4 RxN	. . . .

The end of the optical illusion!

The sound course for Black after *1 B—R3!* is to avoid the pitfall, playing *1 . . . N—N3*, though his position remains difficult.

A really masterly example of a pitfall involving a Pawn offer was seen in the United States Championship of 1946. In the

position of Diagram 144 Black has set up his forces to prevent
P—K4, which would cost White a Pawn. Nevertheless, this move
is highly desirable for White, as it would open up the game fa-
vorably for him. He therefore makes use of a pitfall which is incidental to his plan of opening lines.

STEINER

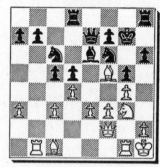

Diagram 144
(*White to play*)

RESHEVSKY

1 P—K4!	. . . .

Black answered this powerful thrust with the bashful reply
1 . . . K—B1. The "wherefore" of this move makes a fascinating
study. Here is what would have happened if Black had gone after
the proffered Pawn:

1	QPxP
2 BPxP	PxP
3 PxP	NxQP

On 3 . . . RxP; 4 B—N2 is devastating.

4 B—N2!	. . . .

This is the point of the pitfall: the long diagonal has been
opened for White's Bishop which was previously skulking on the
back line at QB1.

4	NxB

If Black defends the menaced Knight with his Queen, White forces the removal of the Knight by playing a Rook to Q1.

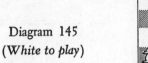

STEINER

Diagram 145
(*White to play*)

RESHEVSKY
(*variation*)

6 N—R5ch . . . .

A murderous move because of the pin on Black's Knight. White wins at least a Rook.

The terrific pressure along the long diagonal explains why Reshevsky set a pitfall with 1 P—K4! and why Steiner hastily removed his King from the embarrassing diagonal with 1 . . . K—B1.

An even more impressive example of a pitfall for power on the long diagonal is seen in Diagram 146.

White is not only formidable on the long diagonal; he also has an open King Knight file, so that his King Rook can aim menacingly at Black's KN2 square.

The long diagonal plus the open King Knight file is an infallible formula for successful attack, so Euwe plays:

KITTO

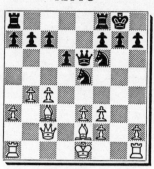

Diagram 146
(*White to play*)

EUWE

1 KR—N1! . . . .

With this charming idea in mind: *1 . . . NxQBP??; 2 BxN(B4), QxB; 3 BxN!, QxQ; 4 RxPch, K—R1; 5 R—N1 mate* (the Rook has five other discoveries on the Knight file that lead to mate).

1 . . . . N—K1

In order to protect the target square KN2.

2 P—B4! . . . .

KITTO

Diagram 147
(*Black to play*)

EUWE

The same pitfall in a second edition. If 2 . . . NxP?; 3 BxN, QxB; 4 BxP!!, QxQ; 5 B—B6 dis ch, N—N2; 6 RxNch mating as previously.

2 . . . .   N—Q2

Now Euwe castled and won in a few moves. Black was completely unnerved by his narrow escapes from disaster.

These few examples prove that seeing the point of a pitfall does not of itself assure salvation. The weight of the position may be against you in any event; or you may see the right plan and choose the wrong method. Now we want to study positions in which a threat or a gimmick is met effectively and thoroughly refuted. The remaining chapters of the book illustrate these methods, and show conditions under which they are likely to meet with success.

CHAPTER 11

One Good Gimmick Deserves Another

Few chessmasters have written as absorbingly about the game as Richard Reti. He rises to heights of eloquence when he explains why sacrificial combinations give us more pleasure than any other kind.

"A combination composed of a sacrifice," he writes in his *Modern Ideas in Chess*, "has a more immediate effect upon the person playing over the game in which it occurs than another combination, because the apparent senselessness of the sacrifice is a convincing proof of the design of the player offering it. Hence it comes that the risk of material, and the victory of the weaker material over the stronger material, gives the impression of a symbol of the mastery of mind over matter."

As you read this passage, you can see that much of it applies to pitfalls, traps, and swindles. Yet if you stop to consider Reti's approach to the whole problem of violent tactics, his ideas seem unreal—not related to a game between *two* players of flesh and blood.

Reti goes on: "Now we see wherein lies the pleasure to be derived from a chess combination. It lies in the feeling that a human mind is behind the game dominating the inanimate pieces, and giving them the breath of life. We may regard it as an intellectual delight, equal to that afforded us by the knowledge that behind so many apparently disconnected and seemingly chance happenings in the physical world lies the one great ruling spirit—the law of Nature."

This is beautifully written, but sadly off key in explaining what makes tactical tricks and finesses work. Any sacrifice, any combination, any gimmick, be it ever so intricate or subtle, *stands or falls by the opponent's reaction.*

Either your opponent plays weakly, in which case your design succeeds; or he plays excellently, in which case your plan fails —to a greater or lesser degree. But in either event your *opponent* has a share in shaping the outcome of the game.

But, you may ask, what of those tactical lines that are so strong that they leave the opposition without recourse? Well, the answer to that still involves your opponent. If you have a forced win, it can only be because your opponent has played badly at some earlier stage of the game. As Reti explains tactical play, you might think it all happened in a vacuum, without the other player having any power to modify the inexorable progress of the attack.

Our view throughout this book is totally different—much nearer to Emanuel Lasker's notion of chess as a struggle between two opponents each striving for victory. Reading Reti and others like him, you gather the impression that good play necessarily wins games, and bad play necessarily loses them.

We can only say that on the basis of experience, good play wins in the majority of cases, and bad play loses. We can add that good play *ought* to win, and *probably* will win. But we must also make allowance for the fact that some players are better than others. Besides, none of us plays with the same degree of skill in every game.

These unknown factors often express themselves through gimmicks—mishandled gimmicks. Diagram 148 involves two amusing examples of putting pieces *en prise*. It is from the Baden gambit tournament of 1914, in which gambit openings were compulsory.

White has played a Danish Gambit and is a Pawn down. Worse yet, he has lost the castling privilege. Indifferent play on his part is therefore to be avoided at all costs; he must try to stir up complications. To that end, he has just played **Q—N3**, attacking Black's Bishop at QN5.

RETI

Diagram 148
(*Black to play*)

NYHOLM

Reti * can defend his Bishop in a variety of ways, but he chooses a really clever method. He plays a developing move which defends the Bishop and also involves a sly pitfall.

$$1 \ldots\ldots \qquad \textbf{N—B3!}$$

White can now win a piece, but he cannot hold on to it.

RETI

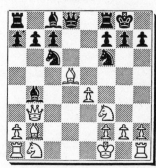

Diagram 149
(*White to play*)

NYHOLM

---

* We have purposely selected an example from Reti's play to belie his own words. Whether his tactical play achieves its immediate goal here will depend on whether or not White is astute enough to see through his opponent's plans!

This is the pitfall: 2 BxQN, PxB; 3 QxB, R—N1!! If now 4 QxR??, Q—Q8*ch;* 5 N—K1, B—R3*ch* and mate in two. And if 4 Q—B3, RxB!; 5 QxR??, Q—Q8*ch* with the same mating pattern.

$$2 \text{ N—B3} \qquad \text{Q—K2}$$

Now the Bishop really had to be defended.

$$3 \text{ P—QR3} \qquad \text{B—Q3!}$$

Again setting a pitfall for White. In the last analysis this pitfall —like the previous one—depends for its success on the fact that White's King has lost his castling privilege. Another important factor, as you will see, is that White's Rooks are disconnected.

In the actual play, White bypassed the pitfall, with this continuation: 4 R—K1 (threatening P—K5), N—K4; 5 NxN, BxN; 6 B—B4, P—B3!; 7 P—KR4, P—QN4; 8 B—K2, B—K3; 9 Q—B2, Q—B4! Black won easily.

Now let us see what Reti's second pitfall was:

RETI

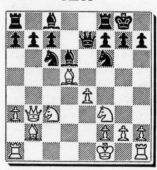

Diagram 150
(*White to play*)

NYHOLM

Had White succumbed to the temptation to try to win a piece, here is what would have happened:

$$5 \text{ BxN} \qquad \text{PxB}$$
$$6 \text{ P—K5} \qquad \text{BxKP}$$

7 R—K1   . . . .

This pin *looks* crushing. But Black has an ingenious resource:

7 . . . .   R—N1!

Counterplay. If now *8 RxB, QxR; 9 QxR, B—R3ch; 10 K—N1, RxQ; 11 NxQ, RxB* and Black's material and positional advantage assures him an easy win.

Or if *8 Q—R2* Black laughs at the pin with *8 . . . B—K3!; 9 RxB, BxQ; 10 RxQ, RxB* again with a position clearly in Black's favor.

8 Q—B2   N—Q2
9 N—Q1   . . . .

Piling up on the pinned piece.

9 . . . .   B—R3ch!
10 K—N1   P—B3
11 NxB   NxN!

He is not afraid of *12 P—B4?* because of *12 . . . N—B6ch!*

12 BxN   PxB
13 QxP   B—N2

Black's position is manifestly superior, and he is still a Pawn ahead. The interplay of ideas here is not only exciting—it is the real crux of the play, and the tactical turns are only secondary, derived from the struggle between opposing ideas.

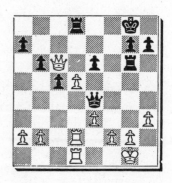

Diagram 151
(*White to play*)

· An even more striking example of putting a piece *en prise* turns up in Diagram 151:

Black threatens mate on the move. White has several ways to defend himself, but the method he selects is certainly the most dramatic: he puts his Queen *en prise!*

1 PxP!!   . . . .

The immediate point of this startling move is to establish White's Queen on the long diagonal, preventing . . . **QxNP mate.**

The second point: if *1* . . . **QxQ;** 2 **RxRch,** Q—K1; *3* **RxQ mate.**

This charming move therefore not only prevents Black from checkmating; it sets up a new mating threat on White's part.

With his Queen and a Rook *en prise*, what is Black to do? If *1* . . . **RxR;** 2 **Q—K8 mate.** With everything lost but honor, Black still has an interesting swindle.

1 . . . .   **RxPch**

Diagram 152
(*White to play*)

Black's swindle is based on the plausible reply 2 **K—B1?** Then comes 2 **RxPch!!** and Black has saved the game. For then *3* **RxR???** allows *3* . . . **RxRch;** *4* **K—K2, QxQ** and wins, or *3* **KxR???,** R—B1*ch!* followed by *4* . . . **QxQ** and wins. Of course, *3* **K—K1???,** **QxPch** leads to mate.*

---

* After 2 **K—B1?,** RxPch*!!* the best line is 3 **K—N1!,** R—N7*ch;* 4 **K—R1!,** RxR dis *ch;* 5 **QxQ,** RxRch; 6 **K—N2,** R—K1 and the outcome is doubtful.

But White has an incisive winning line:

2 K—R1!!!   **Resigns**

Now Black's Queen and both Rooks are *en prise*. None of the discovered checks available to Black can do him any good!

A Queen sacrifice also plays a role in the continuation from Diagram 153. This position was first seen in a famous game between Capablanca and Marshall in the New York tournament of 1918. Black has sacrificed a Pawn for powerful pressure and a considerable lead in development.

MARSHALL

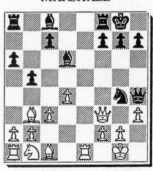

Diagram 153
(*Black to play*)

CAPABLANCA

Black's Rook at QR1 and his Knight are attacked; some kind of drastic action is called for on his part.

1 . . . .   **NxP!?**

Very interesting. If White's Queen wanders far afield with **2 QxR??**, then 2 . . . NxP*ch!* immediately gives Black a winning attack (White's King Rook is lost).

There is a curious pitfall in this position. That Black has left his Queen Rook *en prise* is of little interest to us, but what about Black's advanced Knight? Can that piece be trapped by White?

In the Capablanca-Marshall game, White carefully continued
2 R—K2 sealing the fate of the overdaring Knight.

But more than one player has snapped up the Knight—with
drastic consequences.

2 QxN???   . . . .

HELLING

Diagram 154
(*Black to play*)

STEINER

White has set a pitfall, reckoning on 2 . . . B—N6??? (apparently winning White's Rook on K1); 3 QxPch!!!, RxQ; 4 R—K8
mate! (This mate is impossible while Black's Bishop is at Q3.)

But Black has a gimmick that tops this gimmick:

2 . . . .   B—R7ch!!
3 K—B1   . . . .

To guard his Queen.

3 . . . .   B—N6!
4 QxPch???   . . . .

Now this move is a ghastly blunder.

4 . . . .   RxQch

Unthinkingly assuming that the familiar pitfall was about to
be sprung, Steiner overlooked the importance of Black's 2 . . .

HELLING

Diagram 155
(*Final position*)

STEINER

B—R7ch. The result is that Black is able to capture the Queen with CHECK! White's faulty gimmick cost him the game.

Many a gimmick fails of the intended effect because of a "counter-gimmick" or "in-between move." This novel term is best explained by example, so let us follow the play from Diagram 156.

Diagram 156
(*White to play*)

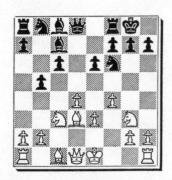

White wants to set up a powerful center with P—K4. But in that case Black can play . . . QxP. Then P—K4 is impossible? No, says White; a gimmick makes it possible. Thus:

1 **P—K4?**   **QxP!**

2 **P—K5**   . . . .

The point of the pitfall. White threatens to win Black's Knight; but, much more important, he also menaces the win of Black's unguarded Queen by **BxPch**. Was White right in thinking he could play **P—K4** safely? The answer is "No" after all, for Black has an "in-between move" disturbing the expected sequence:

2 . . . .   **B—N3!**

The miracle that sets everything straight for Black.

Diagram 157
(*White to play*)

The "in-between move" 2 . . . **B—N3** has saved the day for Black. His Queen is protected by the Bishop; and the threat of . . . **Q—B7** mate gives Black time to save his Knight as well!

Another interesting type of "in-between move" appears when a piece under attack slips away by attacking a hostile unit with gain of time. Such agile squirming has been known to spoil the most ingenious of pitfalls.

In Diagram 158 Black finds that his position is uncomfortable because of White's threatening position on the Queen Bishop file. White has a natural invasion point at QB7, where the action of his Queen Bishop and Queen Rook converges.

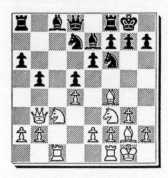

Diagram 158
(*Black to play*)

To shake off the pressure exerted by White's Queen Bishop
and Queen Rook, Black plays:

1 . . . .   N—R4?

Black sees that his opponent has 2 NxQP! in reply, but he has
a gimmick that he thinks will take care of that possibility.

2 NxQP!   . . . .

To Black's way of thinking, White has just stepped into a pitfall. Black is wrong, as we shall see at once.

2 . . . .   PxN

Black expects 3 QxQP? attacking two Black pieces. In that
event Black saves himself with 3 . . . NxB; 4 QxR, NxPch; 5 K

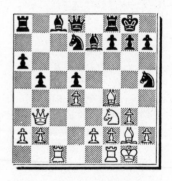

Diagram 159
(*White to play*)

—R1, NxR, which leaves him with a piece for one Pawn. All very neat, but. . . .

3 B—B7!   . . . .

So it is Black, and not White, who has succumbed to a pitfall! Black's reply is forced.

3 . . . .   Q—K1
4 QxQP   . . . .

Black has nothing better than 4 . . . R—R2, permitting 5 **Qx N/R5**, which leaves White two Pawns to the good.

Just as we saw the effect of an interpolated check in the play from Diagram 154, we find that in Diagram 160 an unexpected check ruins what was to all appearances a neat gimmick.

The problem here revolves about a move which at first sight seems altogether out of the question, namely, 1 **RxP**.

Diagram 160
(*White to play*)

1 RxP??!   . . . .

A clever move—or so it seems. If 1 . . . PxR??? Black loses his Queen. And 1 . . . NxR is of course impossible. It seems that White is on perfectly safe ground in relying on the two-way pin. But this illusion is shattered into a thousand pieces by the "in-between" check—

1 . . . .   **Q—R2ch!**

Unpinning the Queen, and therefore winning a whole Rook. This is an effective example of how the priority of check plays hob with preconceived notions.

Even the most persuasive swindles will sometimes be defeated by one artful check, as witness the play from Diagram 161.

Euwe, a former World Champion, has been completely outplayed. He is behind in material and his King is all too fatally exposed.

PALMASON

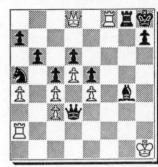

Diagram 161
(*Black to play*)

EUWE

In this game, played in Iceland in 1949, White has managed to concoct an ingenious swindle. Despite his troubles, he is threatening mate, and *1* . . . **RxR???** will not do at all because of *2* **QxR mate.**

White's swindle, moreover, is an extremely attractive one. He offers his Rook on QR2 as bait *that can be captured with check!* This check can be followed up by another check that apparently crushes White. Yet White in turn has an "in-between" check that crushes Black! Here is how the swindle works:

1 . . . .   **Q—N8ch???**
2 **K—R2**   **QxRch**

3 K—N3   B—K3 dis ch

Instead of resigning, White plays:

4 RxRch   . . . .

The "in-between" check!

4 . . . .   BxR
5 Q—B6 mate!

And this might be called the "in-between" mate!

However, this is only a possibility. What actually happened in the game was that Black decided the game at once (Diagram 161) with an "in-between" check:

1 . . . . .   Q—B6ch!!

PALMASON

Diagram 162
(*White to play*)

EUWE

White is caught flatfooted. On indifferent moves Black has 2 . . . QxR or 2 . . . RxR if nothing better offers. But the most delightful alternative is 2 RxQ, when Black, instead of playing the obvious 2 . . . RxQ, has the delectable "in-between" check 2 . . . BxRch, reserving the Queen for capture on the following move. A veritable orgy of "in-between" checks!

You must be particularly wary of such checks if you have not yet castled. The good old maxim is so readily forgotten; *it is easier to menace a King in the center than on the wings.* Black violates this practical rule in Diagram 163 with disastrous results.

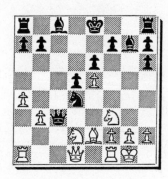

Diagram 163
(*White to play*)

With his King still uncastled, Black has taken time out to snatch a Pawn—a dangerous proceeding, though not yet a fatal one.

1 R—B1!!   . . . .

A sly pitfall. Black's best course is . . . NxNch or . . . NxBch followed by . . . Q—R4. Instead, he dashes headlong for perdition with:

1 . . . .   **QxR??**

Naïvely expecting 2 QxQ??, NxBch; 3 K—R1, NxQ and Black winds up a Rook to the good. But chess isn't that simple!

2 B—N5ch!   . . . .

This "in-between" check comes as a shock to Black. If he plays 2 . . . NxB then 3 QxQ wins, as the Queen is no longer subject to the forking check.

Again, if 2 . . . B—Q2; 3 QxQ and again the forking check is ruled out. After 3 . . . BxB; 4 NxN White has an overwhelming material advantage.

White's "in-between" check has made a miserable hash out of Black's pitfall, leaving him hopelessly behind in material.

Diagram 164
(*Black to play*)

It is clear from such examples that we must be skeptical about seeking complications when the King is still in the center. Yet even great masters violate this rule—sometimes to their sorrow. Reuben Fine came a cropper in one of the most celebrated positions of this kind. Diagram 165 shows the position reached by him in a tournament game played in 1937:

YUDOVICH

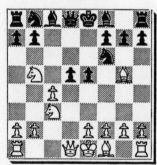

Diagram 165
(*Black to play*)

FINE

Black sets an incredibly refined pitfall with

> 1 . . . .   **P—QR3!**

This is one of those devilish moves that mislead the opponent because he sees them in a context that is familiar—misleading precisely *because* it is familiar!

On the surface, Black's innocent-looking last move is an attempt to drive White's advanced Knight to the unfavorable square QR3. Below the surface, however, *1 . . . P—QR3!* tempts White to set a pitfall that has a serious flaw.

2 NxP??   . . . .

Goaded by his unwillingness to play the unattractive 2 N—R3, Fine is bamboozled into making a faulty combination.

2 . . . .   **PxN!!**

Apparently fatal, but Black sees further ahead than his famous opponent.

3 NxN*ch*   . . . .

YUDOVICH

Diagram 166
(*Black to play*)

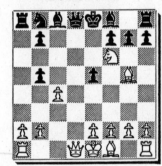

FINE

White has it all—or almost all—figured out. After the expected *3 . . . PxN?* there follows *4 QxQch, KxQ; 5 BxPch* (double attack with check) followed by *6 BxR*. Very ingenious, but he has overlooked the "in-between move"—

3 . . . .   **QxN!!**

Black's gimmick beats White's gimmick!

                4 BxQ   B—N5ch
                5 Q—Q2   . . . .

Belatedly, the crestfallen player of the White pieces realizes
that he has fallen into a subtle pitfall.

                5 . . . .   BxQch
                6 KxB   PxB
                7 PxP   B—K3

With a piece for two Pawns, Black has an easy win.

While the play from Diagram 165 has become famous because
of one amazing move, the continuation from Diagram 167 bristles with cross-purposes and counterplots. In the end Black comes
to grief because he does not take account of the fact that his
King is uncastled. The following position arose in the Beverwijk
tournament of 1953:

SCHELTINGA

Diagram 167
(*Black to play*)

ROSSOLIMO

Black can of course play safe by castling. In that event, White
would have less resources against the coming . . . Q—N3. But
Black plays to counterattack at once, for reasons that we will
have to concede as most compelling.

1 . . . .   **Q—N3!**

This sets up a whole arsenal of threats along the diagonal from Black's QN3 square to the KN8 square. The most dangerous of these threats is 2 . . . P—K4; 3 N—K2, N—Q6 dis ch winning on the spot. (A comical alternative after 2 . . . P—K4 is 3 N—N3, NxN dis ch with wholesale gains of material!)

The more we examine the position the more difficult White's situation appears. The QN3—KN8 diagonal is not the only line along which Black has menacing possibilities. The momentarily veiled action of Black's fianchettoed Bishop also has to be taken into account.

SCHELTINGA

Diagram 168
(*White to play*)

ROSSOLIMO

To get a vivid idea of the power of the fianchettoed Bishop, assume that White carefully removes his King to a "safe" spot: 2 K—R1? In that case, Black wins by 2 . . . N/B4xP!; 3 PxN, N—N5! Now Black threatens . . . N—B7ch winning the Queen, as well as . . . Q or BxN. We conclude, therefore, that 2 K—R1? will not do.

White finds a subtle resource, avoiding Black's pitfall and preparing several on his own account:

2 N—R3!   **. . . .**

Few players would think of this move, as it is almost always considered poor play to develop a Knight to the side of the board. Here the Knight maneuver is of the greatest value. It provides for a later "in-between move"—N—B4—when it is essential to drive off the Black Queen.

Now Black can castle, but he still wants to explore the possibilities of action on the diagonals.

2 . . . .   N—K3

White in turn can play safe with 3 P—B3, but he prefers to seek danger with a move that involves quite a few pitfalls:

3 B—K3!!?   . . . .

SCHELTINGA

Diagram 169
(*Black to play*)

ROSSOLIMO

The first feature of 3 B—K3!! that has a claim on our attention is that it involves the classic theme of offering the Queen Knight Pawn (remember Marshall's story on page 94?).

Here the pitfall is all the more attractively decked out for the prospective victim in that he is allowed to capture the Pawn with gain of time—attacking White's Knight on QR3. Yet, for all that, Black's capture of the Queen Knight Pawn would be fatal—*because of his uncastled state!* Here is the proof: 1 . . . QxP???; 2 N—B4! and Black's Queen is lost after—

I 2 . . . Q—B6; 3 N—N5, Q—N5; 4 P—B3!!, QxN/N4; 5 NxPch! etc.

II 2 . . . Q—N5; 3 P—B3!! and Black has the sorry choice between 3 . . . QxP; 4 N—N5, Q—N5; 5 R—N1 losing his Queen, or 3 . . . Q—B4; 4 NxN with losses of material that are equally punishing.

Black naturally recoils in horror from this pitfall, and sets up some of his own.

3 . . . .   N—N5!!?

This trappy move has many elements of strength, and one possible weakness: *Black is still uncastled.*

SCHELTINGA

Diagram 170
(*Black to play*)

ROSSOLIMO

Black has now reached the maximum of his power, having unleashed an attack on the diagonals of his Queen and of his fianchettoed Bishop. Black's chief threat is 4 . . . QxN!!!; 5 BxQ, BxBch winning material (a Pawn after 6 QxB, or a piece after 6 K—R1??).

The situation is both troublesome and obscure for White. 4 PxN, BxN certainly does not favor him, and 4 P—B3? is altogether inadequate because of 5 . . . NxB; 6 RxN, NxN; 7 PxN, BxP winning.

At first the "in-between move" *4 N—B4* looks promising; but after *4 . . . NxB!; 5 NxQ, NxQ; 6 NxN, BxN; 7 NxR, B—Q5ch* Black has a draw by perpetual check. Yet White, embarrassed for an effective reply as he is, does not want a draw. He wants to maintain the tension and thus maintain his winning possibilities. His solution is:

4 B—N5ch!!?   . . . .

An "in-between" check, taking advantage of the fact that Black has not castled. The rather subtle basic point of this check is that it gives White's King a flight square at KB1 and thus rules out the perpetual check just described. Unfortunately for Black, he does not realize the importance of this finesse.

SCHELTINGA

Diagram 171
(*Black to play*)

ROSSOLIMO

What Black does see, at any rate, is the immediate pitfall: he cannot play *4 . . . K—Q1???* or *4 . . . K—B1???* because then *5 NxNch* wins his Queen. Black's next move is therefore compulsory.

4 . . . .   B—Q2

With several pieces *en prise*, White is ready for the pitfall that has been prepared some moves back:

5 N—B4!?   . . . .

The effect of this "in-between move" is that Black's Queen must vacate the dangerous diagonal—that is, if Black knows what the score is.

Note that 5 . . . QxN?! will not do, because of 6 BxBch, KxB; 7 BxQ, BxBch; 8 K—B1! (the move made possible by the "in-between" check 4 B—N5ch!).

SCHELTINGA

Diagram 172
(*Black to play*)

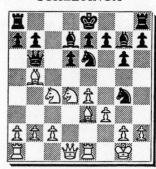

ROSSOLIMO

The right way for Black is 5 . . . Q—B2!

This leaves White's Knight on QB4 in danger, because of the threatened disappearance of the protecting Bishop at QN5. Thus if 6 BxBch, KxB; 7 PxN, QxN and Black stands well.

Likewise if 6 PxN, BxB regains the lost piece.

White's best course seems to be 6 NxN, PxN; 7 BxBch, KxB; 8 PxN, QxN; 9 P—B3 with a difficult game for both sides. *With best play* after 6 . . . Q—B2!, then, Black suffers no ill consequences from his failure to castle. However, in the play that follows, Black's play is not the best.

5 . . . .   NxB?

A one-track mind. Now that White's King has a flight square at KB1, this capture will ultimately leave Black the Exchange down.

6 BxBch!   . . . .

Circumstances alter cases. Now this move is very strong, as Black must reply . . . K—Q1 keeping his Rooks disconnected. (6 . . . KxB??? allows 7 NxQ CHECK.)

6 . . . .   K—Q1

SCHELTINGA

Diagram 173
(White to play)

ROSSOLIMO

In this delightfully confused position in which five pieces are *en prise*, White can win the Exchange by force. Thus his pitfalls triumph over Black's.

7 NxNch   PxN
8 NxQ   NxQ
9 NxR   . . . .

Here 9 . . . B—Q5ch does not draw by perpetual check, as White has 10 K—B1 in reply.

9 . . . .   KxB

After 9 . . . NxP?; 10 BxP Black is even worse off.

10 KRxN   RxN
11 P—B3   . . . .

And White's advantage of the Exchange gives him a technically easy win. A wonderfully instructive example of the power of "in-between moves" and "in-between" checks. Now for a final illustration of this entertaining theme.

Diagram 174
(*White to play*)

Black has deliberately played for this position, which is very far from being as simple as it looks.

Our first impression is that White has an easy win with *1* **RxB**, **KxR**; *2* **B—N5***ch* (double attack with check) followed by *3* **BxR**.

But after *1* **RxB??** Black gleefully reveals his plan: *1 . . . * **RxB***ch!*; *2* **KxR, KxR**; *3* **K—R5, P—N6** and the passed Pawn queens.

Nevertheless Black is wrong, and there is a sad flaw in his pitfall. Here it is:

1 B—B4ch!!!   . . . .

This "in-between" check forces Black's reply—else his Bishop is lost.

1 . . . .   K—B1
2 RxBch!   . . . .

The capture is played with CHECK, forcing Black's hand.

2 . . . .   KxR
3 B—N5ch   . . . .

The third and killing check. White wins the Rook, coming out a piece ahead.

Diagram 175
(*Final position*)

This last example, as well as the earlier ones in this chapter, give us an idea of the power of "in-between moves," checks or otherwise. To break the chain of moves that make a logical sequence is often the prelude to victory; the more startling the break, the more effective the counterattack. This makes a good point of departure for us to consider ways of trumping a gimmick with a better gimmick.

CHAPTER 12

The Trapper Trapped

Because Alexander Alekhine was probably the greatest tactician in the history of chess, it is always interesting to read the comments of his opponents on his style. One significant observation is that, whereas in most tactical sequences it is the *first* move that is the most startling, in Alekhine's case it was the *final* move that was amazing.

It would have seemed less amazing if these commentators had realized the important place gimmicks play in the game of chess. It is characteristic of the gimmick that the last move is the startling one—naturally so, for it is not in the nature of a gimmick that its trappy point be revealed at the start.

But the most startling effects are achieved when one player springs his surprise and finds it topped by a reply even more surprising. As we would expect, Frank Marshall, who was an outstanding master of the gimmick, gives us some of the most delightful examples. One of his neatest efforts turned up in the formidable tournament at St. Petersburg in 1914. Marshall's victim was a master famed for the sharpness of his tactical play.

Black's position inspires distrust on a number of counts. He has not castled, and his Queen's position is insecure. The position of his pieces is inharmonious, and it is not clear how they can be made to cooperate.

On the other hand, Black has pressure on White's backward Queen Bishop Pawn. A master of clever attacking play, Bernstein has worked out a subtle but exceedingly risky plan based on the weakness of the Queen Bishop Pawn.

BERNSTEIN

Diagram 176
(*Black to play*)

MARSHALL

1 . . . .　　　　　N—K5?!

Fastening onto the Queen Bishop Pawn. Marshall accepts the challenge.

2 BxN!　　　　　PxB
3 N—K5!　　　　 . . . .

A real Marshall move. He is not afraid of . . . P—B3, because he is threatening to win Black's Queen with R—N4.

BERNSTEIN

Diagram 177
(*Black to play*)

MARSHALL

Though well aware of the threat to his Queen, Bernstein believes he can afford to disregard the threat. The resource to which he pins his faith is:

3	P—B3?!
4 R—N4	RxP?!

This is the move by which Black stands or falls. If 5 RxQ???, RxR mate, and if 5 RxR, Q—Q8 mate. Apparently Black's incisive appraisal of the situation is quite accurate. He is on the point of extricating himself creditably with 5 . . . Q—B7 in reply to the expected 5 R—R1.

This last comment points up White's major difficulty. He can stop mate, or save the Queen Rook Pawn, or prevent Black's Queen from escaping, but he cannot do all three things at once.

BERNSTEIN

Diagram 178
(White to play)

MARSHALL

Read over the last note again and you may see, as Marshall saw, that there is just one move that answers White's specifications.

5 Q—Q2!!!   . . . .

This is the move that ruins Black's pitfall. His Queen and Rook are attacked, all mating possibilities are stopped, the Black Queen has no escape.

| 5 . . . . | RxRch |
| 6 QxR | PxB |

Acknowledging defeat, but what can he do? If 6 . . . N—N6;
7 Q—B7! is crushing.

| 7 RxQ | . . . . |

White won easily, proving how risky it is to undertake tactical
play when your own camp has vulnerable spots.

The same thought is set forth, in an even more refined form,
in Diagram 179, from the Carlsbad tournament of 1929.

EUWE

Diagram 179
(*Black to play*)

VIDMAR

Black has a fine game, and he can maintain it with the simple
retreat . . . R/B5—B2. Instead, relying on his Bishops and generally greater mobility, he sacrifices the Exchange for an attack
which looks much more promising than it really is.

| 1 . . . . | QxQP?! |

Leading to the forced loss of the Exchange. The line that
Black follows has all the earmarks of trappy time-pressure play.

| 2 B—K4 | RxB |

3 NxR	QxBP
4 NxQP	. . . .

The crucial position. Black stands to lose more material, and now resorts to the swindle which is the logical sequel to his poorly calculated surrender of the Exchange.

4	BxPch?!

Simply playing 5 K—N1 now would quietly set off the hopeless state of Black's game. Instead, Vidmar deliberately falls in with Black's desperate swindle, arriving at a position that seems quite lost for White.

5 KxB!	R—B7ch
6 K—R1	Q—B5

EUWE

Diagram 180
(*White to play*)

VIDMAR

On the surface it seems that White has been gulled into a mating position from which there is no escape. Black has deliberately played for this position—but so has White!

7 R—K8ch	B—B1

Or 7 . . . K—R2; 8 Q—Q3ch picking up the Rook (double attack with check).

8 **RxBch!!**   . . . .

Leading to a spectacular finish which White has had in mind for some time back.

8	. . . .	**KxR**
9	**N—B5 dis ch**	**K—N1**
10	**Q—B8ch!!!**	**Resigns**

For after 10 . . . KxQ; 11 R—Q8 is mate. Black went wrong in giving up the Exchange by *ignoring the weaknesses in his own game*. It is easy to preach that these weaknesses must not be overlooked, but it is not always easy to take the advice. In such positions as Diagram 181, for example, the possibilities are intricate enough to baffle even a seasoned player.

Diagram 181
(*Black to play*)

White has two Pawns for the Exchange, so that material is approximately even. If Black is to seek a win, it must be on some combinative basis. Yet the position of his Rook on KN5 is an awkward one, for it is pinned by White's Queen, with the result that Black's choice of moves is rather limited.

And yet this very pin, which at first sight cripples Black's mobility, may be the winning factor for him. If the pin exists, perhaps it can be broken—violently. For example, is 1 . . . RxPch possible? Obviously White cannot reply 2 PxR, for then he loses his Queen. But on 2 NxR, Black can play 2 . . . QxQ winning the Queen as the Knight is pinned. As it happens, both of these statements are wrong! Nevertheless, on further examination of the position, Black concludes that he can play—

1 . . . .   **RxPch??!**

This loses—but for reasons that are far from easy to discover.

Diagram 182
(*White to play*)

White might be tempted to set a pitfall here that would be ingenious but futile: 2 NxR??? with a view to 2 . . . QxQ???; 3 R—R4ch!! forcing the King to the Knight file so that the Knight is unpinned: 3 . . . K—N2; 4 NxQ and wins!

But Black, with a little foresight, can escape from this pitfall and score a resounding victory after 2 NxR???, RxNch!! There follows 3 K—B1, R—N8ch; 4 K—B2, R—N7ch winning the Queen without having to fear any counterplay from White.

Nevertheless, if you think about it carefully, you will find the clue to White's proper play in these variations.

2 PxR!!!   . . . .

This is the kind of move that stands out in a player's memory after a lifetime of chessplaying! (*See Diagram 183.*)

2	**QxQ**
3 R—R4ch	**Q—R4**
4 RxQ mate	

Diagram 183
(*Black to play*)

In his eagerness to pursue the attack, Black quite missed the
fact that his own King was vulnerable. It was Black's aggressive
policy that led to his King's downfall! Many a gimmick fails
because of weaknesses in the home camp; many others fail because of unjustified reliance on a tactical notion that is almost,
but not always, foolproof.

Pins are often so powerful that it becomes a matter of habit
to think of them as invincible. They aren't. That is the sad dis-
covery that Black makes in Diagram 184.

Diagram 184
(*Black to play*)

Black's position is anything but inviting. His King is uncastled,
his pieces poorly developed, and his Knight at K4 has to retreat.

Instead of giving way, Black tries a desperate swindle which threatens to pin and win White's Queen:

1 . . . .   **P—QN3?**

With a view to **. . . B—B4**, winning White's Queen.

Black will find, however, that there is a flaw in his plan. The pin, powerful as it is, is not a cure-all for all the ills that afflict a position as inferior as Black's.

2 **PxN!!**   **. . . .**

White disregards the threat—and he knows exactly what he is about.

2 . . . .   **B—B4**

A pitfall is a pitfall, Black shrugs. With a piece down, he has no practical alternative to going on with the pitfall.

3 **PxP dis *ch***   **K—B1**
4 **PxP*ch***   **K—N1**
5 **PxR(Q) mate!!!**

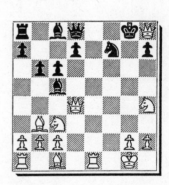

Diagram 185
(*Final position*)

Who said there is no humor in chess! Black's pin is worthless —the White Queen at Q4 is there for the taking, but Black never gets around to it. On the other hand, White's newly promoted Queen "works" because Black's Knight is pinned—and most effectively—by White's Bishop at QN3.

White's pin was powerful because his development was powerful; Black's pin was worthless because his development was worthless.

In the play from Diagram 186 Black is defeated by failure to foresee White's violent breaking out of a pin.

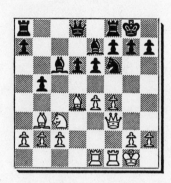

Diagram 186
(*Black to play*)

Black has his eye on White's seemingly vulnerable King Pawn:

| 1 . . . . | P—N5 |
| 2 N—Q1 | NxP??! |

With this line in view: 3 RxN, P—B4; 4 BxPch, K—R1; 5 BxBP, RxB followed by . . . BxR and Black has won the Exchange for a Pawn. All very plausible and ingenious, yet it has a fatal flaw based on an unobtrusive weakness in Black's game.

| 3 RxN | P—B4 |

So far the play has gone according to Black's expectations. But White's next move is an ugly surprise. (*See Diagram 187*.)

| 4 RxP!! | . . . . |

Dramatic proof that Black's pin was worthless. As in the previous example, Black must go through with the trap.

| 4 . . . . | BxQ |

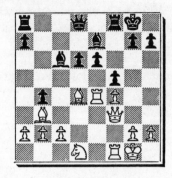

Diagram 187
(*White to play*)

| | 5 RxB dis *ch* | . . . . |

This is what is wrong with Black's trap. He can shut out one White Bishop, but the remaining one becomes even more formidable.

| | 5 . . . . | P—Q4 |

Shudderingly avoiding 5 . . . K—R1???; 6 BxNP mate. And if 5 . . . R—B2; 6 RxR leaves White well ahead in material.

| | 6 RxNP*ch* | K—R1 |
| | 7 R—N6 dis *ch* | . . . . |

Who can blame White for failing to foresee how powerful White's attack would be without the Queen?

| | 7 . . . . | R—B3 |
| | 8 RxR | . . . . |

Threatening R—B8 mate.

| | 8 . . . . | K—N1 |
| | 9 RxB | Resigns |

For R—N3*ch* will be too much for him.

In Diagram 188, too, Black relies on a pin that plays him false. To be sure, Black has earned a drastic punishment by neglecting his development—even to the extent of grabbing the Queen Knight Pawn.

EUWE

Diagram 188
(*Black to play*)

RETI

This game was played in 1920, when Euwe, a future World Champion, was young and inexperienced. Sadly behind in development, he sees a swindle which, so he thinks, will enable him to recover the lost ground.

1 . . . .   NxP?!

An ingenious idea worthy of a better fate—in some other game. Black hopes for 2 RxQ?, BxN pinning and winning White's Queen, and thereby putting an end to White's attacking chances. But White dashes this wistful hope with—

2 NxN!!!   QxRch
3 K—B2   QxR

With his Queen in a deep freeze, Black is powerless to resist the concentrated assault of White's pieces. Black's very considerable advantage in material plays no role whatever. Black's pieces roosting on the last rank have no more than statistical value.

White can recover most of his sacrificed material by 4 N—B7ch and 5 NxR. Instead, commendably despising mere material gain, he weaves an elegant mating net around the lonely Black King. Even though we know Black must fail, his helplessness is astonishing.

EUWE

Diagram 189
(*White to play*)

RETI

	4 BxKP!!	. . . .

Keeps the Black King nailed down in the center, for now flight would be futile: 4 . . . K—B2; 5 N—N5*ch*, K—N1; 6 Q—B4 and checkmate is only a matter of moves.

	4	P—Q3
	5 BxQP	N—B3
	6 B—N5!!	. . . .

Very fine. The removal of Black's Knight will enable White's Queen to penetrate to K7.

	6	B—Q2
	7 BxN!	. . . .

Leaving Black without a good move. (*See Diagram 190.*)
If 7 . . . BxB; 8 Q—K2*ch*, K—Q2 (or . . . K—Q1); 9 Q—K7*ch* and mate next move. Or 8 . . . K—B2; 9 Q—K7*ch*, K—N1; 10 Q—K6 mate!

	7	PxB
	8 Q—K2*ch*!	Resigns

Quite right. If 8 . . . K—Q1; 9 B—B7*ch*!, K—B1; 10 Q—R6 mate.

EUWE

Diagram 190
(*Black to play*)

RETI

If 8 . . . K—B2; 9 N—N5ch, K—N1; 10 N—K7ch, K—B1; 11 N—B8ch dis ch, K—N1; 12 Q—B4ch, B—K3; 13 QxB mate. Note the position of Black's Queen!

In Diagram 191 Black appears to have a reasonably adequate development. Nevertheless, it is not strong enough to support an inadequate gimmick.

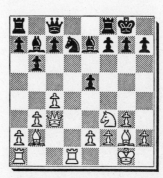

Diagram 191
(*White to play*)

Black has set a pitfall here: if 1 NxP??, NxN; 2 QxN, B—KB3 winning a piece. Unluckily for him, White can adopt a different order of moves with killing effect. White's counterplay begins with a sacrifice of the Exchange:

| 1 RxN! | QxR |
| 2 NxP | .... |

You have to study this move a bit to relish its dynamic qualities to the full. It attacks the Black Queen, of course, but it does much more: it "discovers" an attack on Black's Queen Bishop by White's King Bishop. Also, it opens up a host of momentarily veiled threats on the other long diagonal. Worse yet, Black must reckon with some sacrificial move of the White Knight that will create a mating threat.

| 2 .... | Q—B1 |

To protect his Bishop at QN2.

| 3 BxB | QxB |

A bad spot for the Queen, which has now been forced away from any participation in the defense against White's coming attack. Again and again we have seen in this book how the absence of the Queen from the defense helps the other player execute a crushing attack.

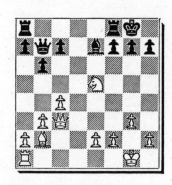

Diagram 192
(*White to play*)

| 4 N—N6! | .... |

Threatening mate and also attacking the Bishop.

| 4 .... | B—B3 |
| 5 N—K7ch! | K—R1 |

6 QxB!!   **Resigns**

For if 6 . . . PxQ; 7 BxP mate. As in the earlier examples in this chapter, Black's inadequate development was not good enough to support the gimmick which he hoped would trap his opponent. Instead, the weakness of his position made possible the "counter-gimmick" that crushed him.

In Diagram 193 we have an even subtler example of the same theme—subtler because White's development is not too grossly inferior, and it takes a really sharp eye to spy out its basic defect.

In this position, which arose in a match game played in 1888, White has the problem of guarding his King Pawn.

LIPSCHUETZ

Diagram 193
(*White to play*)

DELMAR

Protecting the King Pawn presents a problem, for White cannot play P—B4—his King Bishop Pawn is pinned. By the same token, he cannot play R—K1—his King Bishop Pawn needs guarding.

It is a pity that the developing move 1 B—KB4 is not quite satisfactory. After 1 . . . P—N4!; 2 B—N3, P—KR4; 3 P—KR3, P—R5! Black has good attacking prospects. No wonder White seeks an easy way out of his troubles by setting up a pitfall.

1 P—KR3   . . . .

Such a change of pace has often proved useful in a game; instead of fretting over the delicate Pawn, White offers it freely in order to transfer the burden of defense to Black.

1 . . . .   NxKP

Black succumbs to the pitfall—he allows himself to be pinned on the open King file, with his King still in the center. Can he get away with it?

2 R—K1   Q—B3!!

And this seems an outright blunder—protecting a pinned piece with another piece instead of with a Pawn is often fatal. Greatly heartened, White puts more pressure on the pinned piece.

LIPSCHUETZ

Diagram 194
(*White to play*)

DELMAR

3 Q—K2   . . . .

Most players would consider Black lost. On 3 . . . B—Q3 the precariously placed Knight is lost at once by 4 P—B4.

What else remains? At first sight Black seems to have a clever resource in 3 . . . B—Q5, which guards the pinned Knight while still staving off the catastrophic 4 P—B4. But even here

White has a refutation in 4 B—K3!, BxB; 5 QxB winning the Knight—or 4 B—K3!, BxN; 5 PxB. Now Black's Knight is unpinned, but Black is lost all the same.

For example, if 5 . . . Castles; 6 B—Q4! setting up a new pin and winning the Knight. And on 5 . . . NxB there follows 6 B—N5 dis ch, Q—K3; 7 QxN with a new pin that wins Black's Queen.

So it seems that whatever Black does he is crushed by some disastrous pin. However, it would be all wrong to accept this as an impressive indication that White's pitfall is effective. It can be refuted—but how?!

LIPSCHUETZ

Diagram 195
(*Black to play*)

DELMAR

3 . . . .   **Castles!**

A "simple" solution.

Instead of laboring with might and main to guard the threatened Knight, Black gives up the piece. It goes without saying that this sort of stratagem cannot be recommended for any and all positions. There has to be a logical reason for relinquishing a piece like this.

In this case the logical reason is *the existence of a weak point in White's position*—at his KB2 square. Again we see that a player cannot expect his pitfalls to be effective when he has weaknesses in his own camp.

4 QxN . . . .

White can renounce his intentions and refrain from capturing the Knight. In that event he has lost a Pawn without the slightest compensation.

    4 . . . .   **QxPch**
    5 K—R1   . . . .

If 5 K—R2, B—Q3 pinning White's Queen—and this is a pin that works!

    5 . . . .   **BxP!!**

It is really this second sacrifice that proves White's undoing. How is he to stop the threatened mate and continue to protect his Rook at K1?

LIPSCHUETZ

Diagram 196
(*White to play*)

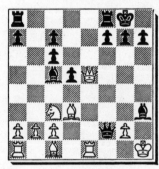

DELMAR

White has many moves in this position, but none of them are any good.

For example: 6 B—B1 or 6 R—K2 allows 6 . . . **Q—N8 mate.** On 6 Q—R2, Black checkmates beginning with 6 . . . **QxRch.** If 6 Q—K2, BxPch; 7 K—R2, B—Q3ch leads to quick mate.

The weakness of White's KB2 square led to a new kind of weakness—the split in White's forces which prevents them from working together.

| 6 PxB | Q—B6ch |
| 7 K—R2 | B—Q3 |

Wins the Queen.

| 8 QxB | . . . . |

A last hope—after 8 . . . PxQ White has three minor pieces
for Queen and several Pawns, with some chance of dragging out
his resistance for a while.

LIPSCHUETZ

Diagram 197
(*Black to play*)

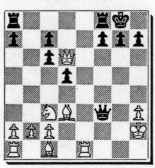

DELMAR

| 8 . . . . | Q—B7ch! |

A pleasant example of the "in-between" check. The White
Queen is *en prise* and won't run away. Meanwhile Black picks
up the unprotected Rook with check.

| 9 K—R1 | QxRch |
| **Resigns** | |

One of the most convincing examples of a gimmick that is
faulty because of a weakness that robs it of any sting.

Now one more example—this time a Knight fork—which
fails because of a hidden flaw.

White is ahead in development and thinks he has an effective
way of turning this lead in development to good use.

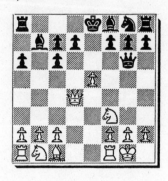

Diagram 198
(*White to play*)

1 P—K6?!   . . . .

Very tricky. 1 . . . QxKP??? is not a good defense against the
mating threat, for then 2 R—K1 pins and wins the Queen.

But 1 . . . Castles will not do either: 2 PxQPch, RxP?; 3
QxRch!, KxQ; 4 N—K5ch followed by 5 NxQ and White has won
the Exchange.

1 . . . .   · BPxP!!

A refined reply which prepares a diabolical refutation of
White's pitfall.

2 N—K5   . . . .

Diagram 199
(*Black to play*)

Playing as planned. White threatens mate and attacks the Queen. Black's position is ripe for resignation—or so it would seem.

2 . . . .   **QxPch!!!**

The proverbial bolt from the blue.

3 KxQ   **P—B4 dis ch!**

This sly sequel to Black's previous "in-between" check wins White's Queen, leading into an ending in which Black is two Pawns to the good. There is something irresistibly comical about the abrupt way Black's apparently buried Bishop comes to life.

In this last example, as in all the earlier diagrams in this chapter, we have seen how the existence of a fundamental weakness spoils gimmicks that might well be effective in a sound position. Spot your opponent's weakness and you will turn many a hostile pitfall to your own advantage.

CHAPTER 13

Thrust and Counterthrust

By now you can appreciate what an important role gimmicks play in chess. They contribute enormously to the game's richness and variety. They give us a lasting assurance of novelty without which the game would soon pall, as everything does that is foreordained and predictable.

Chess gimmicks are the enemy of the banal and the lazy. They hold out hope for the almost defeated, and key up the almost victorious player to his best efforts. Gimmicks have been the secret of many a success—and likewise many a failure. They are not always easy to find, but they are always worth looking for.

To conclude our study of gimmicks worthily, we shall enjoy a glance at some of the finest examples in the whole range of chess literature. For sheer ingenuity and amazing variety of ideas, it would be hard to improve on the following illustrations.

The first one is from the World Championship match of 1929, a thrilling struggle between two tactical wizards.

Black's King is insecure, but his two extra Pawns offer some consolation. Should he succeed in beating off the attack, he will win easily by advancing his two connected passed Pawns. Consequently Alekhine must seek complications—the more the better. While his pieces are aggressively posted, his prospects of direct attack look none too bright.

But Alekhine finds a way!

BOGOLYUBOV

Diagram 200
(*White to play*)

ALEKHINE

1 NxP!   . . . .

Winning back one of his Pawns, for *1 . . . NxN??; 2 B—K4*
would be deadly.

1 . . . .   Q—N6!

A powerful counterattacking move, for after the natural reply
2 R—R3 Black forces the exchange of Queens with a won ending. (Until White finds a way to establish material equality and
break the power of the passed Pawns, the exchange of Queens
means a lost game for him.)

2 Q—KB1!   . . . .

Very fine. He guards the Bishop, staves off the exchange of
Queens, and preserves tactical possibilities for his Queen.

2 . . . .   N—Q4!

Bogolyubov's last move sets an ingenious pitfall. It seems to
expose Black to the loss of a piece, but will actually net him
complete simplification, if White is unwary.

Thus, after *3 B—QB4* Black's Queen must move, allowing
4 BxN, BxB; 5 R—Q6ch winning a piece.

But Bogolyubov has it all figured out: on *3 B—QB4* he plays

BOGOLYUBOV

Diagram 201
(*White to play*)

ALEKHINE

3 . . . Q—N8!!; 4 BxN and now 4 . . . QxQch!!; 5 KxQ, B—QN4 ch! (double attack with check) winning White's Rook and compelling exchanges.

3 R—R1!	B—QN4!!

He is not afraid of 4 R—N1, to which he has the "in-between" reply 4 . . . BxB!; 5 RxQ, RxR! picking up the Knight as well with a winning advantage in material.

4 BxB*ch*	QxB
5 Q—K1!	. . . .

It is curious that this back-rank maneuvering can produce a strong attack. The Queen is headed for KN3.

5	Q—B3
6 Q—N3	Q—KN3
7 Q—R3	. . . .

With nasty threats of discovered check.

7	K—B3

Apparently the safest refuge, but just what Alekhine wanted! He makes good use of the seemingly disjointed position of his pieces.

BOGOLYUBOV

Diagram 202
(*White to play*)

ALEKHINE

8 NxPch!!	. . . .

A typical Alekhine surprise. Now he has established material equality, and Black still has several chances to go astray.

8	PxN
9 Q—B8ch	B—B2
10 R—B1ch	. . . .

Black can easily go wrong here. If now 10 . . . K—N3; 11 B—R5ch! he does best to return the piece at once with 11 . . . K—R2! If instead 11 . . . KxB???; 12 QxR or 11 . . . K—R3??; 12 Q—R8ch! R—R2; 13 QxN!! (not 13 R—B6ch??, K—N4!!) and White's double threat of 14 R—B6ch and 14 BxB wins for him.

Bogolyubov, who has thoroughly mastered the complexities of the situation, adds a new wrinkle of his own:

10	N—B6!!
11 BxN	. . . .

Black's last move looks suicidal, for if now 11 . . . PxB???; 12 RxPch, K—N3; 13 R—N3ch and wins. But Bogolyubov has an "in-between move" that saves the day.

This surprising resource must have been calculated on the previous move.

BOGOLYUBOV

Diagram 203
(*Black to play*)

ALEKHINE

11 . . . .   R—N8!!

By pinning White's unguarded Rook, Black takes the sting out of B—R5 dis *ch* which would otherwise be murderous.

At the same time Black sets a pitfall: *12 B—Q2 dis ch?, RxRch; 13 BxR, Q—N8!* This new pin wins for Black, as after *14 Q—K8ch, K—N3!; 15 Q—K1* Black has still another pin with *15 . . . B—B5.* Then after *16 B—Q2, QxQch; 17 BxQ, P—Q6; 18 K—B1, P—Q7; 19 BxP, BxB* Black has won a piece.

12	Q—R8ch!	K—Q2
13	Q—R4ch!	K—B1
14	B—Q2	RxRch
15	BxR	. . . .

Alekhine has successfully avoided the last pitfall, for if now *15 . . . Q—N8; 16 Q—K8ch* White draws by exchange of Queens after *16 . . . K—N2; 17 Q—K4ch:* or by perpetual check after *16 . . . B—Q1; 17 Q—B6ch, B—B2; 18 Q—K8ch* etc.

15 . . . .   Q—Q3

The game was abandoned as a draw several moves later. A superb example of resourceful play by two master tacticians.

Equally entertaining is the ingenious swindle that saved Teichmann a few years earlier in the Carlsbad tournament of 1923:

TEICHMANN

Diagram 204
(*Black to play*)

ALEKHINE

You will recall Teichmann from an earlier discussion. On this occasion he manages to fool even the great Alekhine.

The situation shown in Diagram 204 is well-nigh hopeless for Black. He has material equality, but positionally his game is as good as lost. His backward Queen Bishop Pawn is a lasting target for White's pieces, and his Bishop is condemned to immobility. With continued passive play on his part, his defeat is assured: White will double Rooks on the Queen Bishop file and eventually the pressure will become unbearable.

In positions of this kind, a swindle is often the only hope of saving the day. Teichmann's swindle is exceptionally slick:

1	P—QR4!!

This swindle is a good one, even psychologically. It offers White a Pawn, but on two conditions: that he do away with the backward Pawn, and that he weaken his King-side. (There is, as you will see later, a third condition—that White, having won the Pawn, will be unable to hold on to it; but it will take some time before even Alekhine realizes that.)

The swindle is a good one, then, because it subtly undermines White's self-confidence. Enjoying the initiative, his motto was "full speed ahead." Now, as a result of Black's swindle, he is preoccupied with problems and plagued by alternatives.

                              2 PxP?   . . . .

Alekhine fails to see the full point of the swindle and therefore plays to win the Pawn. With 2 R—B2 he would have maintained the pressure.

                      2 . . . .   PxP

Suddenly Black's Bishop comes to life!

                      3 QxNP   . . . .

If he plays 3 BxB to avoid weakening his King-side, 3 . . .
QxB saves the Pawn. But, as Black is not geared for a King-side
attack, what harm can there be in a slight weakening of White's
King-side position?

                      3 . . . .   BxB
                      4 PxB   R—Q4!!!

This move embodies a threat so subtle that very few players
would even be aware of it. Black threatens a perpetual check
beginning with 5 . . . QxPch!!!

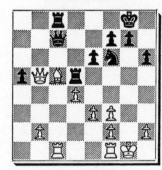

TEICHMANN

Diagram 205
(White to play)

ALEKHINE

Black threatens 5 . . . QxPch!!!; 6 KxQ, R—R4ch; 7 K—N3,
R—N4ch; 8 K—B4, R—B4ch; 9 K—N3, R—N4ch etc. with no escape from the checks.

If White tries 5 Q—Q3, there follows 5 . . . QxPch!!!; 6 KxQ, R—R4ch; 7 K—N3, R—N4ch; 8 K—B4, N—Q4ch!! (not 8 . . . R—B4ch??; 9 QxR!); 9 K—K4, N—B3ch still drawing by perpetual check as the White King's flight to Q3 has been blocked. This finesse is the basic point of the whole swindle.

5 P—B4   . . . .

This stops the perpetual check, but Black has by no means shot his bolt.

5 . . . .   **N—K5!**

By attacking the pinned Bishop Black threatens to regain the lost Pawn.

6 R—B2!   . . . .

A skillful parry. If 6 . . . NxB; 7 KR—B1! and the pin on the Knight leaves White a Pawn ahead.

6 . . . .   **P—N4!!**

And this is the finesse which assures Black of regaining his Pawn.

TEICHMANN

Diagram 206
(*White to play*)

ALEKHINE

7 P—B3!	NxB!
8 KR—B1!	R—N1!
9 Q—K2	PxP
10 PxN	PxP

Black has regained his Pawn, and the game was given up as a draw several moves later.

An equally gallant try for a draw appeared in a game played at Berlin, 1928:

SPIELMANN

Diagram 207
(*White to play*)

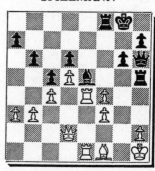

RUBINSTEIN

With a powerful King-side attack already built up, Black threatens to decide the game by . . . BxP. White's position is desperate and probably lost, which inspires Rubinstein to conceive a really heroic swindle:

| 1 P—R3 | BxP |
| 2 Q—K2! | . . . . |

Spielmann now reached out to play 2 . . . RxPch??, having in mind the continuation 3 BxR, QxBch; 4 K—N1, R—B4 and White can resign. Suddenly he took his hand away from the board and after some moments of agitated thought he played 2 . . . B—K4, winning in another twelve moves or so.

What was wrong with going through with the original combination as planned?

SPIELMANN

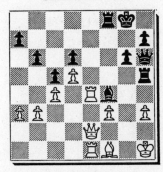

Diagram 208
(*Black to play*)

RUBINSTEIN

Here is what would have happened if Spielmann had been taken in by the swindle:

2	. . . .	RxPch??
3	BxR	QxBch
4	K—N1	R—B4???
5	R—K8ch!	K—N2
6	Q—K7ch!	K—R3

"And wins"—but at this point Spielmann noticed, to his horror, that White has—

7	QxKRPch!!!	KxQ
8	R/K1—K7ch	K—R3
9	R—R8ch	K—N4
10	RxQ	. . . .

And White wins! But, as we have pointed out, Spielmann avoided the swindle in good time.

In the following example, from a game played at Helsinki in 1938, White was less fortunate:

NIEMI

Diagram 209
(White to play)

RASMUSSEN

White plays to win a Pawn—a singularly unfortunate experiment. He is headed for trouble because his Queen Bishop is still at home, which makes communication between his Rooks impossible.

1 NxNch   . . . .

Apparently forcing 1 . . . NxN if Black is to avoid loss of a Pawn.

1 . . . .   BxN!

This unexpected way of recapture ought to be a warning to White.

2 PxP   . . . .

It isn't.

2 . . . .   NxP
3 BxPch??   KxB
4 Q—B2ch   N—Q6!

Now we see why Black played 1 . . . BxN! Still, it seems unbelievable that he can avoid losing the Knight.

5 R—Q1   B—R3
6 N—K1   . . . .

NIEMI

Diagram 210
(*Black to play*)

RASMUSSEN

Can Black's bedeviled Knight, pinned two ways and attacked by three pieces, hold out against the pressure?

6	**Q—B1!!**

Tricky. He returns the pinned Knight, but after 7 **QxQ, QRxQ**; 8 **NxN, KR—Q1** he pins on his own account and wins *White's* pinned Knight. (The fact that White's Rooks are not connected tells heavily against him.)

7 **Q—N1!**	**R—Q1!!**
8 **NxN**	**K—N1!!**

What has happened here is characteristic of positions where a player tries a gimmick though handicapped by inadequacies in his own position. He works hard to win the Knight, only to find that his troubles have really begun after regaining the Knight.

Black threatens to win the pinned Knight with . . . **Q—Q2**. What can White do about it? Precious little, as a glance at Diagram 211 indicates.

White's helplessness is pathetic. He cannot budge his Queen Rook, Queen, or Queen Bishop, nor can his Knight move out of the pin. An instructive possibility is 9 **P—B3, Q—Q2**; 10 **N—B2, QxRch!**; 11 **NxQ, RxNch**; 12 **K—B2, B—Q6!** trapping White's Queen and remaining a Rook ahead.

NIEMI

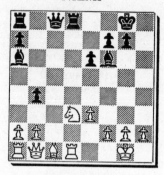

Diagram 211
(*White to play*)

RASMUSSEN

| | 9 P—KR3 | . . . . |

Justified despair.

	9	Q—Q2
	10 Q—B2	BxN
	Resigns	

In Diagram 212 a pin also plays an important role; but it is overruled by a promotion theme with several pretty points.

COLLE

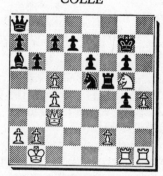

Diagram 212
(*White to play*)

STOLTZ

In this game, played in the Bled tournament of 1931, Stoltz

has outplayed his opponent magnificently. Now the time has arrived for quieter play, and the simple 1 P—N3 would easily maintain a decisive advantage. But, overcome by the excitement of the struggle, Stoltz is carried away by his desire to win brilliantly.

He would like to play 1 R—K1, piling up on the pinned Knight. But after 1 . . . K—N1!; 2 RxN? would be answered by 2 . . . QxRch. In order to rule out this possibility, Stoltz plays—

1 P—B4??   PxP e.p.

The foregoing variation has now become impossible, but at the cost of creating a Frankenstein monster in the form of Black's powerful passed Pawn.

2 R—K1??   . . . .

COLLE

Diagram 213
(*Black to play*)

STOLTZ

White now has the position he wanted, and looks forward confidently to these variations:

2 . . . P—Q3; 3 NxPch, K—B2; 4 NxP, Q—N2; 5 NxB, QxN; 6 PxP and Black is lost.

2 . . . K—B3; 3 RxN!, RxR; 4 R—K1, P—Q3; 5 NxBP and Black's position is on the point of collapse.

Nevertheless, Black has at his disposal one of the finest swindles ever conceived. The play that follows is remarkably deep.

2 . . . .   **P—B7!!!**

This move is bewildering in its appearance of inadequacy. It is obvious that White can win with 3 RxN, QxRch???; 4 R—K1 **dis ch** winning Black's Queen.

3 RxN   . . . .

Why not?

3 . . . .   K—N1!!!

This quiet retreat wins the game!

4 R—KB1   Q—N7!

Obvious, though the sequel is anything but that.

Belatedly White realizes that he is in trouble, for if 5 Q—B1, RxR with the winning threat 6 . . . QxR!; 7 QxQ, R—K8ch etc. Or if 5 Q—KR3, RxN!; 6 QxQ, RxQ; 7 R—K2, BxP and wins, for if 8 R/K2xP, BxR! or 8 R/B1xP, R—N8ch! (an "in-between" check).

5 Q—Q3   . . . .

COLLE

Diagram 214
(*Black to play*)

STOLTZ

White's pitfall is just a bit too obvious: 5 . . . RxR???; 6 QxNPch and mate next move.

To lift this mating threat, Colle plays a spectacular move—

5	BxP!!
6 QxB	RxR
7 Q—Q3	. . . .

Threatening mate.

7	QxRch

Puts an end to White's daydreams, for after 8 QxQ, R—K8ch ends it all. This is swindling of a very high order!

The Barmen tournament of 1905 produced a duel with an even more varied set of tricky motifs in a short sequence of moves:

ALAPIN

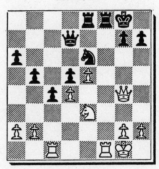

Diagram 215
(*White to move*)

MAROCZY

The possibilities in this position are actually much more complex than appear at first glance.

The Pawn position tells us most of what we need to know about the likely course of the play. Black has three Pawns to two on the Queen-side. If the forces are reduced to the endgame stage, this Queen-side majority can be converted into a passed Pawn with a likely win for Black.

On the other wing there is a struggle for control of the King

Bishop file, complicated by the fact that White's passed King Pawn is strong, while his Queen Pawn is weak. These items serve as clues to the following play.

1 N—B5!   . . . .

The first pitfall, inviting Black to win a Pawn by *1 . . . NxP???; 2 QxN???, RxN* etc.

Actually, the reply to *1 . . . NxP???* would be *2 N—R6ch* winning Black's Queen!

1 . . . .   R—Q1

Black protects his Queen in order to be able to play . . . NxP. White's logical course is to double his Rooks on the open King Bishop file; how he should go about this is something of a problem; there is one sure way to double, and several wrong ways to do so.

ALAPIN

Diagram 216
(*White to play*)

MAROCZY

One wrong way to double the Rooks creates an amusing trap: *2 R—QB3??* (intending *R/B3—B3*), *NxP!!; 3 N—R6ch, K—R1; 4 RxRch, RxR; 5 QxQ, N—K7ch; 6 K—R1, R—B8 mate*.

To avoid this trap, White tries to double Rooks in a different way:

2 R—KB3?   . . . .

A mistake. 2 R—KB2! is correct, for a reason that will become clear.

2 . . . .   RxN!

Taking advantage of White's mistake. White cannot reply 3 QxR, NxP!; 4 QxQ because of 4 . . . NxRch! ("in-between" check!); 5 PxR, RxQ with an easy endgame win based on the extra Pawn. (This explains why White should have played 5 R—KB2! ruling out the "in-between" check.)

3 RxR   NxP!

ALAPIN

Diagram 217
(*White to play*)

MAROCZY

White must give back the Exchange—if 4 R—B4? (or 4 R—N5?), QxQ; 5 RxQ, N—K7ch winning a Rook and coming out a piece ahead.

4 R/B1—B1   NxR
5 RxN   Q—R2ch
6 K—R1   Q—K6

Black has won a Pawn and should win the game. The presence of the Queens gives White some drawing chances. A remarkably intricate sequence, considering the apparent simplicity of the position in Diagram 215.

For our final example we take a game from the Scarborough tournament of 1927 which bristles with trappy moves. Most of the moves made from Diagram 218 were made under great time pressure. The improvisations and misjudgments of both players may be traced back to their lack of time for clear thinking. The result is a fascinating series of superb traps, threats, parries, and swindles.

YATES

Diagram 218
(*Black to play*)

BUERGER

Black is the Exchange and a Pawn down, and in the ordinary course of reasonably tranquil play there is not the slightest doubt that he will lose the game. The ordinary requirements of sound play no longer apply for him, for sound play will not suffice to hold the position. His only chance is to swindle, and keep swindling. This preliminary explanation, plus the time pressure, will tell us much about the following play that would otherwise seem wildly irrational.

1 . . . .   **P—Q6!?**

To open up lines for his pieces.

2 P—B4!   . . . .

Creating a new crisis for Black. If he retreats the menaced Knight, he will lose another Pawn. If he plays 2 . . . PxP; 3 QxP and then retreats the attacked Knight, White will exchange Queens and then win the Queen Knight Pawn. So Black arrives at a desperate resolve. To create complications, he offers the sacrifice of several pieces with—

2 . . . .   N—Q5!?

YATES

Diagram 219
(*White to play*)

BUERGER

Pressed for time, White ought to be seeking ways to simplify the situation. A good way would be 3 P—K3, N—K7ch; 4 K—N2, NxR; 5 BxN, NxP; 6 QxP and though White is only a Pawn ahead after giving back the Exchange, he should win with little trouble.

3 PxN!?   . . . .

This should also win, but it requires the most exacting mastery of the coming complications.

3	PxP/K7
4 PxR	PxQ(Q)
5 PxQ	Q—K7
6 QR—K1	. . . .

Black has a Queen for two Rooks and a Pawn—a Pawn that is just about to queen. Though it seems that Black ought to resign on the spot, he has quite a few swindles at his disposal.

YATES

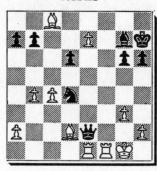

Diagram 220
(*Black to play*)

BUERGER

6 . . . .   **N—B6ch!**

This Knight must be captured because of Black's mate threat.

7 RxN   B—Q5ch

Though Black is teetering on the edge of defeat, he is putting up a magnificent fight. White has only one move to avoid an immediate loss.

8 B—K3   QxR/K8ch
9 K—N2   Q—K7ch

Black's swindles have achieved what we may expect of every good swindle—changed an easy win into an arduous one. White has a far from easy choice here because of the perpetual checking possibilities. Thus 10 R—B2? will not do because of 10 . . . QxB; 11 R—B7ch, B—N2; 12 B—Q7, Q—K7ch and Black draws.

10 B—B2!   . . . .

So that if 10 . . . QxKP; 11 BxB Black has removed the terrible

Pawn at the cost of leaving himself with a hopeless inferiority in material.

10 . . . .   BxB!

YATES

Diagram 221
(*White to play*)

BUERGER

Now White is actually behind in material, but he can still win!

11 R—B7ch!   . . . .

To answer this move with *11 . . . K—R1* will not do because of *12 B—N4!!* followed by R—B8*ch* and P—K8(Q).

However, note this swindle: if *11 . . . K—R1; 12 R—B8ch??,* K—N2; *13 P—K8(Q)*, B—K6 dis *ch* and Black draws!

11 . . . .   K—N1!?

Trickier than *11 . . . K—R1* because by attacking the Rook Black "hypnotizes" his opponent into giving the following check. Once White gives the check, he can no longer win.

It is White's misfortune that he is too pressed for time to reason logically about the position. In order to win, he must queen his Pawn in a position where Black's perpetual check is ruled out. The only square from which Black's Queen can threaten perpetual check *and* restrain the Pawn from queening

YATES

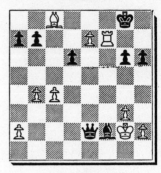

Diagram 222
(*White to play*)

BUERGER

is K7. This is also the only square from which the Black Queen
can give perpetual check *after* White's Pawn queens.

What all this adds up to is that White's only winning move
is *12 B—K6!!!*

First point: if *12 . . . QxB; 13 R—B8ch, K—N2; 14 P—K8(Q)*
winning, as Black has no perpetual check.

Second point: if *12 . . . B—K6 dis ch???; 13 R—B2 dis ch* winning Black's Queen!

Third point: if *12 . . . B—B4 dis ch; 13 R—B2 dis ch, QxB;
14 R—B8ch, K—N2; 15 P—K8(Q)* and once more Black has no
perpetual check.

12 R—B8ch?   . . . .

Time pressure and the swindles have befuddled White. Now
he has no more than a draw.

12 . . . .   K—N2
13 P—K8(Q)   B—K6 dis ch!

The only move to draw. White cannot escape from the checks.
(*See Diagram 223.*)

14 K—R3   Q—R4ch
15 K—N2   Q—K7ch
Drawn

YATES

Diagram 223
(*White to play*)

BUERGER

This is swindling in the grand manner!

About the Authors

I. A. HOROWITZ, *editor and publisher of* Chess Review *since 1933, has been one of America's outstanding chessmasters for more than twenty years. He has won the United States Open Championship three times, and he played on the winning American teams in the International Team Tournaments at Prague, 1931; Warsaw, 1935; and Stockholm, 1937.*

FRED REINFELD *is credited with being the world's most prolific chess writer. He has also defeated many of America's leading masters in international competition. After annexing the Intercollegiate Championship in his undergraduate days, he won the New York State Championship twice and subsequently became the titleholder of both the Marshall and Manhattan Chess Clubs.*